PUBLISHERS ™

CREATIVE TEXTS PUBLISHERS
PO Box 50, Barto, PA 19504

Creative Texts Publishers products are available at special discounts for bulk purchase for sale promotions, premiums, fund-raising, and educational needs. For details, write Creative Texts Publishers, PO Box 50, Barto, PA 19504, or visit www.creativetexts.com

DISASTER IN THE BURBS
by Jerry D. Young
Published by Creative Texts Publishers
PO Box 50
Barto, PA 19504
www.creativetexts.com

ISBN: 978-0692433621

DISASTER IN THE BURBS
By
JERRY D. YOUNG

CHAPTER ONE

-

Darlene wrestled the polymer barrel onto its stand beside the other five. A whole house cistern would have been so much better, but she hadn't been able to get a variance to install one. The particular suburb she lived in was like that. Even with water shortages in the news almost every day, they wouldn't let her, or anyone else, install a cistern. At least they didn't deny her the barrels. Possibly because she hadn't mentioned them to anyone. Darlene smiled as the thought crossed her mind.

It had taken some careful planning and design work to get the gutter and downspout system installed so it would come to a single discharge into the first water barrel. There was a diverter just above the barrel and a trash filter just above that. The six barrels were connected together at the bottom, with a long frost proof faucet in another tee in the pipe.

Darlene worked the rest of the day building the thickly insulated enclosure for the barrels. She didn't want them to freeze in the winter. With the job done, Darlene stepped back and looked at the total package. "Not bad, if I do say so myself," she said. The custom gutters and downspouts matched the color of the house nicely, as did the paint on the wooden, foam insulation board lined, enclosure. Now all she needed was some rain.

Tired, but happy, Darlene went back into the house, ready for a light supper, a shower, and some sleep. She needed to go in early to work the next morning and was tired from the past two days of working on the house and lot.

Early the next morning, dressed in one of her office outfits, Darlene grabbed her BOB and went outside to the five-year-old Subaru she had bought after selling the new Lexus that became hers in the divorce. The Lexus had been Steven's idea of an appropriate car for his wife. And he had the money to pay for it.

She set the BOB in the back of the Subaru next to the tote that contained emergency equipment for the Subaru. It also held some supplies if she got stranded for some reason and decided to stay with the Subaru rather than try to make it home using the BOB and the folded up Montague Paratrooper bicycle next to the tote.

Getting in and starting up the Subaru, Darlene looked at the house and smiled. She'd caught a good deal and picked the house up from a seller desperate to sell. He even financed the small balance remaining after she put down a whopping down payment, using the money she'd received from the divorce for her share of the house she and Steven had lived in while married.

The house, though it boasted three bedrooms, two baths, and a two car garage, was very compact, with all the rooms, except the kitchen, on the very small size. Over all it was less than half the square footage of Steven's not quite mansion. She sure didn't miss keeping that house clean.

The house had been just what she was looking for. It was in a gated community. Though the house was relatively small, the lot was large, so the house was set well back from the street, but still left lots of backyard.

There were no alleys, so all the utilities were out in the street. The back of the property was fenced with an eight-foot high chain link fence, with green colored slats in the weave. Plenty of privacy from the back door neighbor.

Though the development hadn't included side fences the way they had the rear fences, many in the community had put in their own. A few even had decorative front fences. Darlene had already made arrangements with both side neighbors to put in privacy fences between her and them, on a shared cost basis. They would match the rear fence, with privacy slats in the fence from the back fence up to the point even with the front of the houses. The decorative front fence would wrap around and meet the chain link fence. Short fences, also with privacy slats, would connect the side fences with the corners of the house, a gate on each side.

The smile still on her face, Darlene pulled out of the driveway and headed for the gate of the small subdivision. There were for sale signs here and there, for houses, vehicles, and various 'toys,' such as boats, quads, and snowmobiles. Times were getting really tough. That was part of the reason she'd 'downsized' her life, after being 'downsized' out of the marriage at Steven's insistence. Well, more Roberta's insistence, as Steven had seemed to be fine with having both a wife and a mistress. Though she would have left the marriage, anyway, when she found out about Roberta, Steven filed first.

Darlene would have liked to have just told Steven to stick the divorce settlement, but couldn't bring herself to give him that satisfaction. He would have jumped on the offer. As it was, he fought tooth and nail to get out from under as much of the divorce settlement he could.

Waving at Bear, the guard at the gate, Darlene slipped her sunglasses on and pulled out onto the main street through this section of the city's large suburban tract. Glancing at the clock in the Subaru, she slowed down after merging into traffic. No need to hurry. She was still plenty early.

It took another fifteen minutes to get to the offices of Blain and Sons Rock & Iron Works. She parked under 'her' tree, and went to open up the office. When Stanley Blain and his boys, Ricky and Ted, got there, the coffee was brewing, the donuts were set out, and the payroll was finished, the checks ready for Stanley's signature.

"Hey, Beautiful!" Stanley said as he poured himself a cup of coffee, "When do you want us to start on that fencing for you? Things are slow. Be a good time to do it." He leaned against the reception counter and took a sip of coffee. The boys grabbed handfuls of donuts and disappeared into the shop.

"I'm on a budget, Stanley. No money at the moment for the fences."

"Yeah. How about the neighbors? I'd be willing to do it if they can pay their shares and wait on yours for a while."

"Oh, Stanley… I don't know. I don't like owing. I'm out of debt, except for the house payment and don't want to add any. Not the way the world is going right now."

"Well, considering that, a woman alone, fences would be comforting, I would think." He gave Darlene a wink and headed back to the shop after the boys. Work was slow, but they still had some jobs to do.

Darlene shook her head. Stanley was right. Even in the gated community, security fencing would make her feel better. And the Association had already approved the side fences and a decorative front fence on her lot. She had to grin again. The Association members had been happy with the decorative fence. She had presented it as such, but in reality it was also a security fence. Just a very good looking one. Stanley had a good eye for design.

The front fence planned would be a low rock wall with wrought iron between rock posts. There'd be a remote control wrought iron gate for both the driveway and the walkway. Darlene was getting the fencing at cost plus from Stanley. Making up her mind to talk to her neighbors that evening, Darlene set about her work.

The next morning a delighted Darlene spoke to Stanley as soon as he came in the door of the office. "That fencing? The neighbors want to do it. And the riots have decided them to get fences on the other side of their houses, and a front fence each, too. Nothing like mine, but it's paying work."

"Good work, Beautiful. With the company discount and work finder's fee, you aren't going to owe all that much."

"I didn't do it to get a finder's fee, Stanley!"

"I know that. But I don't want to lose you. You're about the only woman that will put up with me in the office. Ever since you came to work here, I haven't had a misquoted order, lost shipment of material, or late paychecks. I want you safe and sound in that house of yours."

"Stanley!"

"We'll start as soon as the granite countertop is finished for the Cushman house. I wish I could bring back a crew, but I just can't justify it right now."

There was no arguing with him once he'd made up his mind. His head was as hard as the rocks and iron he worked with. Darlene was going to have her fencing. Much sooner than planned.

"Okay, Stanley. Thanks."

"Sure thing, Beautiful." Stanley headed back into the shop and left Darlene to her work.

Darlene kept an eye on the TV in the office for news updates as she processed invoices. Things were tough all over and getting tougher. During her lunch break, Darlene checked her bank account balance over the Internet and made a few calculations, based on the new, lower cost of the fencing.

Knowing the money she was earning was losing value every minute she held it, Darlene decided to up the speed she was preparing her home for the even worse times she thought were coming.

A project she'd been saving for, a small propane powered automatic generator, backed by a small solar power system for critical electrical circuits, would now be top priority. The automatic start generator produced 3.4 kilowatts of power, was in a very quiet enclosure, and used two 20-pound propane tanks, thereby negating the need to try and get a variance for a permanent propane tank. Which she was very unlikely to get.

She would get longer hoses for the propane bottle connections so she could use one-hundred pound tanks for much longer running time before refueling. There was no specific restriction against them, and what the Association didn't know wouldn't hurt her. She planned to get three of the one hundred pound tanks, to keep two connected and one to rotate into the filling rotation.

The power distribution cable with GFCI outlets would be replaced with a regular automatic transfer switch that would interface with the solar power system.

The solar power system would be the costlier of the two units, using a few 315-watt RWE-Schott 48-volt solar panels, a Xantrex/Trace inverter set up, and six Surrette 8-volt batteries. The use of solar panels wasn't clearly defined in the Association CC&R's, and at least one tenant in the subdivision had been denied a variance for a large array system for its 'unsightliness.' With the back of the house facing the south, giving perfect light for the panels, they wouldn't be in sight from the street anyway. Again, what the Association didn't know wouldn't hurt her.

Using the company buying power, as Stanley encouraged her to do, she ordered the components. It almost cleaned out her account, but she had just been paid and hadn't deposited that check yet. She'd have money to live on, but that was about it for a while.

The following weekend Darlene got back to work on one of her ongoing projects that she'd let go for the time as she was putting the water barrel system put in. She'd picked up another six 8"x8"x16" concrete blocks, a sack of mortar mix, and a few sacks of Quikrete.

Darlene was turning the second bay of the two-bay garage into a storm and fallout shelter. It was a basic box built of the concrete blocks mortared together and filled with the Quikrete mixed, like the mortar, in a wheelbarrow parked in the garage. The blocks had rebar every layer and every other concrete filled vertical cavity in the blocks.

When she got to that point, the roof of 4"x6" beams spaced every 12", covered with two layers of ¾" plywood, would have solid concrete blocks mortared into place, again with rebar tying the roof together with the walls.

Darlene started building it right after she'd moved in. Now, what she considered the back wall of the shelter was complete, with the side walls stepped from the full height of that wall to the floor. The back wall was two-feet from the side wall of the garage. The end wall facing the garage door almost touched it. The other end wall was two feet from the back wall of the garage. That two feet of space around two sides of the shelter would be boxed in with removable panels, for secure storage.

To have room to access the top of the shelter to install the roof, the inside roof height was only six feet. The inside open area would be six feet wide by sixteen feet long, not counting the space in the baffle wall at the entrance. Darlene normally did six to twelve blocks each weekend, scoring the concrete already in place and treating it to get a good seal with the fresh concrete she added to the blocks she placed on that lift.

With the six blocks in place, the mortar and concrete setting up, Darlene started another project that would take a little while. A more distant project was a greenhouse built against the back wall of the garage. She wanted a well installed before the greenhouse went up around it.

Hiring the work done would draw too much attention. The water table in the area was only eight or nine feet down, and a local that jetted shallow wells in told Darlene that driving a screen point and pipe down twenty-five to thirty feet would get her at least some water.

She considered hiring him to do it, but again, it wasn't something she wanted broadcast to the neighbors. So, with the five-foot, inch and a quarter screen point, five five-foot lengths of inch and a quarter threaded galvanized pipe, drive rated couplings, a drive cap, a can of pipe dope, two pipe wrenches, and the old driver that Jim, the well driller, had rented to her, Darlene set to work.

The point went into the soil quickly and easily. She added a joint of pipe, put the drive cap on it, and managed to get the driver over the pipe. She got that section driven almost three feet deep, giving the pipe a right hand turn every little bit to keep the joint tight, before she simply gave out, her arms like rubber. Besides, she didn't want the dull thumping sound to last long enough to get the neighbors curious.

The parts for the backup electrical system came in as Stanley was wrapping up the fencing job. Darlene hired Stanley's boys to help with the installation of the solar panels and the batteries. Very heavy batteries. Between the instructions that came with the equipment, and some research on the internet, Darlene had the system up and running two weeks after the fence was finished.

As riots in the city became more commonplace, nearly every weekend now, as prices of food and fuel went up, Stanley's business began to boom. Residential areas were being hit as well as the downtown area. Those that had much of anything to protect, wanted the protection.

Stanley gave Darlene a small raise, and a generous bonus when residents in the same gated community Darlene lived in came to the shop to see about similar fencing. The company name plate was on the fence and Stanley got a total of fifteen more orders in the community.

Darlene took the money she'd been saving up for a greenhouse, put it with the bonus, and got a greenhouse one size larger than she'd planned. She wasn't ready to put it up yet, but with inflation running nine percent, she didn't want to hang onto the money very long.

With the raise, and the overtime Darlene was now getting, she upped her preps even more. Using the various swap papers and classifieds, Darlene began shopping for something to protect herself with. Her father had been a shooter, but her brothers got the few guns he'd had when he died.

Prices were high, despite the economy. At least, some of them were. Wanting something soon, Darlene set her sights a bit lower than she had initially. And, it turned out, a bit more PC than the 'black' rifles and semiauto pistols she'd been considering. The need for long range shooting was limited, in her circumstances, so she decided to forgo that requirement and look for something powerful, even if short range.

She found the ad in one of the shopper magazines. A woman was selling off her recently deceased husband's small collection of guns. No prices were given with the listing of the firearms. Only two caught her eye. A Marlin 1894 stainless steel lever action rifle in .44 Magnum and a Ruger Redhawk, also in .44 Magnum, with five-and-a-half-inch barrel, also in stainless steel.

Her father had owned one of the Rugers at one time, but had sold it before he died. Darlene had shot it a couple of times with full power .44 Magnums and hadn't liked it very much. But with .44 Specials, it was a different story. The Ruger and Marlin both used the .44 Magnum and .44 Special interchangeably. The magnums wouldn't be any problem at all in the rifle, but she could keep the Redhawk loaded with .44 Specials, but still use the magnums in it if needed.

Darlene didn't waste any time, going to the address straight from the grocery store where she'd found the paper. It didn't take long to cut a deal. The woman threw in all the accoutrements her husband had for the two guns. Along with the Marlin and Ruger, Darlene got a pair of western style leather bandoleers, each with sixty loops for the .44 cartridges, and a leather gun belt and holster for the Ruger that had six pouches containing speed loaders for the Redhawk.

She took the guns to the local range that Sunday and tried them out. The rifle was fine, but the grips of the Redhawk were too large for her hands. They were custom grips and Darlene was able to order a set of Pachmayr Decelerator grips for it that would fit her hands much better and perhaps make the use of magnum shells a bit more comfortable.

Darlene picked up three five-hundred-round cases each of .44 Special and .44 Magnum before leaving the range shop. Feeling much more capable of protecting herself and her home, Darlene went home and put in a couple of hours on the shelter and the well before she called it a day, ate supper, took a shower, and went to bed.

That was what her life was like for the rest of the summer. After the heat wave early, that had probably been part of the cause of the riots, since there had been brown-outs and black-outs, the summer had finished up fairly mild, and the rioting had pretty much disappeared. But no matter where you went in the city and even out in the suburbs where Darlene lived, tensions were high. An announcement that it would be a hard winter, with shortages of heating oil, propane, and natural gas, had people growling and grumbling about not only the availability, but the nearly tripling of cost.

Darlene had been buying a one-hundred-pound propane tank and two forty pounders each paycheck since she got the three for the generator. Her house was on natural gas, but if the flow stopped, she wanted to be able to use campers' style inside-safe propane heaters to keep enough heat in the house to avoid the pipes freezing, and run a camping stove to cook on.

At work, Darlene was having to deal with delinquent accounts on a regular basis. Stanley was getting the work, but people weren't wanting to pay the going price. And Stanley had kept his prices as low as he could and still make a decent profit. The business began to slow down even faster than it had picked up. Without the riots keeping peoples interest up in securing their homes, fences were secondary to fuel and food.

Food prices were rising every month, for a variety of reasons, which really didn't matter too much to those unable to afford the limited amount that was available. People just knew that the shelves were more empty than full, and the prices were the highest on record.

Darlene saw the handwriting on the wall. She didn't make Stanley hem and haw for a while before he had to tell her he had to let her go. She went into his office after finishing the payroll for that week to give Stanley the checks to sign and to talk to him.

"Stanley, you have to cut expenses. You can no longer afford me. You're down to one crew, plus you and the boys. You'll have to do the office work yourself, to save money."

Stanley sighed. "Aw, Beautiful, I'm trying to find a way to keep you on. It's just... You see the books..."

"That's what I'm trying to tell you, Stanley, I don't work here anymore, after today. It'll help if you give me a pink slip showing a layoff, rather than me just quitting.

That way I can, maybe, get some unemployment, if I can't find another job right away."

"If things turn around, will you come back? You're the best thing that's happened to this place in a long time."

"I will if I can, Stanley. I promise. If I've found a permanent position, it wouldn't be right to leave them to come back here."

"I understand," Stanley replied, with a rather larger sigh.

Fighting back tears, Darlene went back to the reception desk and began making notes about how she did her work. What she did, when, and why. At the end of the day, after she gathered up her few things in the office, she stepped into Stanley's office to say good-bye.

He nodded, stood up and gave Darlene an awkward hug, and handed her an envelope he'd been turning around and around in his hands when she entered.

"Something you need me to mail on my way home?" Darlene asked with a smile. It wasn't an unusual errand for her to do.

"No. No, Beautiful. It's your severance."

"I got my check," Darlene replied.

"No. This is in addition to your final check. Here."

Darlene set the box down with her things in it and opened the unsealed envelope. "Oh, Stanley! You can't afford this!" She tried to hand the check back to him and he sought the protection of his desk between them.

"Yes, I can. Now go on before one of us starts crying." Stanley sat down and dropped his eyes to the desktop.

"Thank you, Stanley," Darlene finally said, adding the envelope and check to the box she picked up before she turned and left, tears slowly rolling down her cheeks.

It certainly wasn't like she couldn't use the money. She could. She only had enough left in the bank to pay the house payment and eat for the rest of the month. The check would allow her to pay off the house, since there were only three double payments more to get the deed. She'd been paying double the agreed upon rate from day one.

She took care of that task the following day, and then had the Subaru serviced and bought the supplies to have it done five more times, fearful she wouldn't be able to afford it later, and even wondering if the supplies would even be available later. She bought the place out of the oil she used, as well as the filters.

Darlene went home and looked around the place, making decisions on what to use the rest of the money, before it lost value. Other than some for emergencies, and immediate future needs, she intended to invest all the rest of it in a manner to make the coming times easier.

Besides the greenhouse, she wanted a regular garden. The previous owner had grown a small one in the back yard and Darlene intended to do the same, on a larger scale. To make it as efficient as possible, Darlene checked the yellow pages for small engine repair shops and went looking for a good used rototiller.

She came back not only with a Troy-built rototiller, but almost everything else she needed in the way of hand tools to put in a garden. The only things the little shop didn't have, rather surprisingly, were fuel cans. After unloading the tiller and the tools, Darlene attached the small basket carrier that plugged into the Subaru's receiver hitch and went to get jerry cans and fill them up.

It took her several trips to get all the fuel she felt she could afford, and picked up spare parts for the tiller, to boot, including oil, sparkplugs, and drive belts, storing everything in the existing yard shed near the back fence that had come with the house.

Darlene held onto enough of the money to buy the remaining supplies to finish the shelter. The rest went to a plan that she decided was better not to ask the Association about. There were plenty of rabbit breeders around, and Darlene had no problem getting hutches, a buck and three does. Having read on the internet about raising fish in a barrel, she searched the internet to find the information.

After reading through it, she went to the closest farm supply place, which wasn't very close at all, and bought the largest polymer stock tank she and the clerk could shoehorn into the back of the Subaru with the hatch open.

When she got home she quickly backed the Subaru into the open bay of the garage and unloaded the tank. No need to advertise to anyone passing on the street. She waited until she had set up a worm farm under the rabbit hutches before she filled the tank with water and stocked it with tilapia fish. The fish would be fed the worms that fed on the rabbit droppings.

The last of the money went for the materials to build a chicken coop and tractor, though she didn't assemble it, much less get chickens. That, even under current circumstances, would bring the Association down on her.

With winter coming on, and no job, Darlene put up the greenhouse, with a little free help from Stanley and his sons. She quickly got a garden started in the greenhouse, and then tilled the ground in the back yard that would be a garden the next spring. She wanted it tilled so it would absorb all the moisture they received during the winter.

With a few of her planned projects still pending, Darlene went looking for work, signing up with the temporary service that had placed her at Stanley's, where he'd hired her direct, after the required time with the temp service.

She got some work, but not much. But since she was getting some, she got no unemployment benefits. Feeling guilty about the large severance check Stanley had given her, she volunteered to do the payroll, the most difficult of programs for Stanley to use, for no pay. Strictly volunteer.

Stanley protested, a little, but finally accepted her offer. Having let the last crew go, for lack of work, it was only Stanley and the boys now. Though the amount of work wouldn't support two crews, it kept Stanley and the boys busy six days a week. Stanley, despite not being very good at the paperwork the business generated, didn't have time, either.

Darlene slipped in a little more work than just payroll. Neither she nor Stanley said anything about it. With only twenty to thirty hours a week through the temp service, Darlene still had plenty of time to do the work for Stanley, and still work on her prep projects.

With only enough income to buy groceries and a little gasoline for the Subaru so she stayed mobile, most of the prep work was minor stuff. Work in the greenhouse, and taking care of the rabbits and fish. The worms pretty much took care of themselves.

One other thing she did was set up her sewing machine and get back into practice sewing by making several items of clothing for herself with the fabric she had on hand.

Going from the wife of a moderately wealthy man to a single woman on her own wasn't as much of a shock to her system as it would be to some. She'd grown up in a family that had to make do during her formative years, and the lessons had stayed with Darlene.

She watched as neighbors held yard sales in the development, selling anything and everything they could, to help make ends meet as prices kept going up quickly, and salaries went up slowly, if at all.

Along with the yard sales she was seeing, Darlene also saw 'For Sale' signs going up in the yards of several of the houses in the development. Times were really getting tough. Then the blackouts started in earnest. There had been occasional blackouts and brownouts during the summer, but with winter coming on, the expectation had been they wouldn't occur again until spring, after the last two-hour blackout the week before.

They didn't bother Darlene much. The solar power system was working like a charm and kept her refrigerator, freezer, furnace, computer, and a few lights going. Other than the monthly exercising of the generator, Darlene had not used it since she'd installed it. It was quiet enough not to alert the neighbors to its presence, but Darlene decided not to run it unless the battery bank got too low for efficient operation.

Darlene, having read much of the PAW fiction on the internet, made sure that no light showed when the commercial power was off. Besides the fiction she'd read, there had been several incidents reported in the local news of generators being stolen, and accounts of aggressive neighbors in some places demanding the use of someone else's generator because they needed it worse than the generator owner.

Preferring to keep a low profile, Darlene made it appear she was in the same boat as all her neighbors. It would be hard to steal her generator, but she didn't want the neighbors on her doorstep asking to run an extension cord to their house, or to store frozen food in her freezer.

She was particularly careful after talking to Jayne Noodle and her husband, Kevin, her east side neighbors, one evening when both drove up at the same moment and spent a few minutes talking through the fence.

Jayne was complaining about the blackouts and, because of them, loss of some meat in her freezer. She came right out and said, "I sure wish there was someone close with one of those electrical makers. I'd be first in line to store some things from the freezer in theirs. I think they would have an obligation to do it, don't you?"

"Gee, I don't know, Jayne. Don't you think they'd have their own problems to deal with when the power is out?"

"Well, probably. But it would be the neighborly thing to do," Jayne replied.

Darlene bit her lip to avoid saying anything else. She did decide to jibe her neighbor just a bit, though. "Are you guys considering getting one?"

"Heavens, no! They're noisy and people steal them. We aren't about to put up with that kind of aggravation and risk. I do wish someone would get one close though." Jayne grinned. "But not too close to have to listen to that noise. Though… What about you? You going to go out and splurge so I can keep the steaks frozen? Maybe I could stand the sound."

"I'm afraid I couldn't afford it now. I'm not getting much work," replied Darlene, not willing to lie, but not willing to tell Jayne that she already had a generator.

A week later, it was announced that there would be rolling blackouts scheduled for the foreseeable future. That was bad in and of itself, but without power, the overwhelming majority of tenants in the tract were not able to run their heating systems, since the natural gas heaters were electronically controlled. Three days before Christmas the natural gas was cut off for the first time. The district had been cut off to provide the limited supply of natural gas to colder areas. The temperature the first night was right at freezing. Even when the power was on, those heating with natural gas didn't have heat, for lack of natural gas.

Propane and kerosene portable heaters disappeared almost overnight, just as had generators when the blackouts were scheduled. The small portable bottles of propane were gone shortly after the propane heaters, and the larger tanks, the 20's, 30's, and 40 pounders shortly after that. Propane was still available and Darlene filled the two 20 pounders she'd emptied after their initial purchase.

To top it off, California was deep in the midst of a drought, along with many other places, and fresh foods were becoming scarce. Foreign imports, especially from South America, while available on the docks, weren't being shipped in due to the high price of transport, which would have put the cost of the imports out of reach of many Americans, anyway.

Unusual for winter, especially in twenty-degree weather, a riot broke out at one of the big chain grocery stores in the city. It seemed to be a spark. Grocery stores all over the area had rioters out front, protesting both high prices and lack of availability for even basic foodstuffs. Three stores had the doors broken after they were locked due to the riots, and people made off with what food was available.

Even the store Darlene and many of the others in the subdivision used was mobbed. And it wasn't inter-city gangs, or ethnic minorities that did it. It was the suburbanites in the area. Darlene was at home, watching the news, when that incident occurred. A news team happened to be close when it started and were filming people leaving the shop in droves, carrying things in their hands. Darlene sat up suddenly. One of the looters looked like Jayne!

Stepping out her front door, Darlene looked to see if Jayne's car was at home. Jayne and Kevin had the bad habit of leaving their garage doors open. Neither of their vehicles was there. It could have been Jayne in that TV clip. Darlene shook her head and went into the house.

It was perhaps an hour later when the walk gate alarm went off. Darlene jumped up and took a look outside. It was Jayne walking up the walkway to Darlene's front door. She was carrying a grocery bag in one hand, holding her coat closed against the cold weather with the other.

Darlene stepped outside. "Jayne? What's going on?"

"I... uh... bought some things without paying attention to what I was picking up. Things Kevin and I don't eat. I was checking to see if you wanted them. Perhaps had some good steak or even ground beef you'd mind trading for."

"Gee, Jayne," Darlene said carefully, "I don't eat much beef any more. I don't think I have any in the freezer."

"Would you check?" I hate to see food go to waste. And if you don't eat it much anymore, it would only be right for me to take it off your hands."

Reluctantly Darlene said, "I'll check."

Darlene didn't know how to prevent it when Jayne followed her into the house when Darlene turned and went inside. "Oh, my! It's warm in here!" Jayne immediately said. Darlene hastily went into the kitchen, opened the freezer door grabbed her last one-pound package of ground beef, and closed the door, loudly, immediately coming back into the living room.

Jayne was looking around. When she looked back at Darlene after seeing the enclosed space safe propane heater sitting in the hallway, facing the living room, there was a mixture of suspicion, anger, and even a little hurt, in her eyes. "You have a propane heater! Kevin and I were too late to get one." It was much more an accusation than it was simple statement.

Darlene nodded. "Here. I did have some ground beef left."

Jayne took it, and thrust the grocery bag at Darlene, and turned toward the front door. As she stormed out, she said, loudly, "You should be ashamed! It's just not fair!"

Stunned slightly at the vehemence in Jayne's voice, Darlene hurriedly closed and locked the front door. Then she looked in the grocery bag. Suddenly she shook her head. A jar of cocktail onions and two cans of clam juice. Darlene thought to herself, "She didn't even know what to loot! Gee Whiz! I wonder if she even looked to see what she was grabbing."

Shaking her head, Darlene carried the items into the kitchen and put them away. She didn't know when she'd ever use them, but she wasn't going to throw them away. To take her mind off things, Darlene went out to the greenhouse to do a little work. But first she activated the remote controls for the driveway gate and the sidewalk gate. She should have been locking them anyway, but for sure they would be locked from now on when not being used.

Things just kept getting worse for most. Darlene was doing well, with enough income to keep fuel in the Subaru, and pay the gas, electric, telephone, and cablevision bills, and still keep a bit of cash available for emergencies.

Many in the tract weren't doing anywhere that well. At least three families she was aware of had just walked off from their houses, unable to pay the mortgage, and provide the necessities. There were hopes that spring would bring better times. Congress was working on a comprehensive plan to get the economy under control, and do something about the shortages of critical items.

One of the early steps taken was the recall of all bullion gold, silver, platinum, palladium, and rhodium in private and commercial hands. Darlene smiled when she heard the announcement and unconsciously touched the belt she was wearing with her jeans. It had a zippered compartment in it that contained a few of the US Gold Eagle one-tenth-ounce coins she had.

After the divorce, Darlene had sold all the jewelry that Steven had bought for her and liked her to wear so he could show her and it off. The money had all gone into the bullion coin purchases, made at various coin dealers with cash, and without names. She wouldn't be turning in any of what she held.

The enforcement of the recall was hit and miss. So much of the precious metals had been sold without records, that tracking them down was difficult and the government didn't spend too much trying to enforce it. Not only were individuals refusing to pony up the goods, some sellers turned in a bit, to make it look good, and then did a land market business buying and selling on the black market.

The next thing the government did was institute price and wage controls. Fully a third of what was available of just about every commodity went into the black market that sprang up overnight.

Things were now harder to get, at the controlled prices, than before the controls. And since there was a real shortage of the items, the black market prices were sky high. But at least some people had the money to buy, for the black market was a going concern. What little she bought, Darlene bought at the regular outlets, paying the controlled prices. When something was available.

It so happened a shipment of food was scheduled at the closest grocery store one Friday. Darlene had been riding the Paratrooper bicycle whenever the winter weather permitted and the distance wasn't beyond her ability. She took the bicycle when she went to the store early that Friday. There was already a line to get in, and Darlene locked up the bike and took her place at the end.

Jayne, who had been giving Darlene the cold shoulder since the incident in Darlene's house, drove up right after Darlene and got in line behind her, without speaking to her. Darlene decided to try to mend fences, so to speak, and to break the ice, said, "It's nice to have the power and the natural gas back on for a few days, isn't it? And a shipment of food. I feel blessed."

"Well, I don't. This is America. I shouldn't be standing in line to get a loaf of bread and a can of tuna!"

"Why don't you shut up?" said the woman in front of Darlene. "You ought to be thankful you're getting anything at all. Look at you. Dressed to the nines, and I saw that Mercedes you drove up in. Spare me the indignation. I'm surprised you aren't buying on the black market, a hoity-toity woman like you."

Darlene thought Jayne was going to explode and attack the woman. But when the woman mentioned the black market, it seemed to sap Jayne's anger and trigger her curiosity. "I heard about the black market on the news, but that's just in the city center isn't it? Cigarettes and booze?"

"Honey, you need to get out more. See that guy standing over there by the closed down pizza place?" The woman nodded her head in the direction to one side of the line. "That's the black market, at least today. Whatever they've got here in the store, he probably has three times that much. But he isn't selling it for the price control price, I can guarantee you. Believe you me, if I had the juice, I'd be buying from him."

"Really?" Jayne asked, her eyes on the man with interest. "Excuse me." With that, Jayne left the line and headed for pizza shop. Darlene watched her neighbor talk to the man for a few seconds and then go into the shop. The windows were all covered on the inside with newspaper.

Darlene still had not made it to the front of the line when Jayne came out of the pizza place carrying two grocery bags. The way she was carrying them they looked to be full. Darlene just shook her head and took another step forward as the woman in front of her was allowed into the store.

Darlene, when it came her turn, picked up only a few things. For three reasons. She felt a bit awkward taking some of the limited stock that was available, didn't have much money to spare, and there wasn't that much to buy, anyway.

After strapping the cotton grocery bags she'd brought with her to the bicycle, she unlocked it, climbed on, and pedaled home. The next week Darlene arrived earlier than she had for the first rationed delivery.

There was less there at the start than when she'd been allowed in the previous week. She just couldn't bring herself to take any of the food. There were several women there with children. Buying what she wanted would be taking that food out of those children's mouths. At least that was the way Darlene looked at it.

What she did take was several of the free community newspapers from the racks in the entryway of the store. As she left the supermarket Darlene saw Jayne's car at one of the small shops in a nearby strip mall. Though she couldn't really tell for sure, the man standing outside the closed down beauty shop looked to be the same one at the pizza shop the previous week.

She was sure of it when she and Jayne arrived home at the same time. Jayne pulled up to the one of the garage doors and stopped the car. She took out two paper grocery bags and hurried into the house with them.

After storing the bike in the garage, Darlene went inside and fixed herself a cup of tea to help warm up some. Though she was dressed well for the weather, riding into the wind on the way back from the store had chilled her face, and even her hands through the gloves she wore.

Sitting down at the kitchen table with the mug of hot tea, Darlene opened up the first of the three community papers she'd picked up. It was sad. People were trying to sell all manner of things; some Darlene was sure they really didn't want to.

She had some specifics in mind and quickly went through the papers. There were only a couple of submissions that fit her wants. People who had chickens wanted to keep them. There were plenty of entries for people selling eggs and dressed chickens, but only the two for live chickens. She filed away the information for future use.

The weather broke the next week, and Darlene tilled the outside garden again, getting it ready for planting. Her cell phone rang perhaps twenty minutes into the work. It was Jayne. "Is that you making all that noise?"

"Uh… Well… I'm tilling my garden, but…"

"I'm reporting this to the Association!" Jayne said and hung up.

Barely finished cleaning up after the chore was done; the buzzer for the front gate rang. Darlene looked outside and saw the Association president, Jake Harlan, the secretary, Brenda Coombs, and Jayne standing at the gate. The buzzer went off three times in rapid succession before Darlene could get to the door to go outside.

When she got to the walk gate she made no move to open it. "What can I do for you?" she asked through the tall spiked bars of the gate.

"We need to come in and talk to you," Jake said. "There's been a complaint."

"We can talk here," replied Darlene coldly. "I take it that this is about the rototiller."

"You have no right to make that much noise," Jayne said. "It's against the CC&R's."

"I'm afraid she's right," Brenda said. "I have a copy of the CC&R's right here and it says…"

"I know what it says," Darlene said, cutting Brenda off. "It says that no nuisance noise over… I don't know, several decibels, I can't remember exactly how many, but it's moot. I was not generating nuisance noise. The noise is being produced by an accepted activity. Namely, gardening. It's exempt from the noise rules, unless it is in the dangerous level. Which the tiller isn't."

"Let me see that book!" Jayne said. But Jake took it before Jayne could.

After a minute of silence as Jake read the applicable section, Jake snapped the book closed and turned to Jayne. "She's within the rules." He turned away and headed for his car. Brenda went with him.

"I'm sorry the noise bothers you, Jayne. I'll try to limit it to times when you're gone."

"Well, I guess if you can't afford to feed yourself, you have to make do. Look at you. You're wearing suspenders just to hold up your pants! How much weight have you lost?"

"I'm doing okay," Darlene replied.

"Of course you are, dear. You just go right ahead and use that noisy machine. I'd hate for you to starve to death."

Jayne went down the sidewalk and turned into her own walk gate.

Darlene had to hide a smile. Despite the condescending tone and words, Darlene's deliberate wearing of her old 'fat clothes' had done what she intended. Disguised the fact that she was, in fact, maintaining her weight and not losing any the way many people were. Darlene had noticed that even Jayne, with her black market purchases of food, had lost a bit off her already slender frame.

Going back into the house, Darlene decided to go ahead and keep the tiller use to times when Jayne was not home, if at all possible. The less Jayne thought about Darlene, the better.

CHAPTER TWO

-

Spring went well and Darlene's garden flourished, as did the greenhouse garden. Her rabbits were breeding nicely, as were the fish. She had the freezer full of rabbit, fish, and vegetables. To earn a bit of extra money, she began taking her excess to a local farmers' market that had sprung up during the hard times.

She turned the money right around and invested in dwarf fruit trees for the back yard. Before she planted any in the front yard, which was on her mind, she went to see Jake and Brenda to see if planting trees in the front yards was against the CC&R's. It wasn't. In fact, it was encouraged.

Of course, Darlene knew Jake was talking about stately shade trees and beautiful ornamentals. But the CC&R's didn't specify what kind of trees. Darlene bought several more fruit trees, plus a few nut trees, for the front yard.

Darlene watered the garden and newly planted trees heavily, when needed, using the collected rain water and water from the hand pump on the well she'd driven. The yard sprinklers were on city water. When summer rolled around, with only a few showers during the spring, water rationing was in effect before July 4th and Darlene quit watering the lawn. She continued to water the garden and trees with water from the hand pump.

She watered by hand, carrying the water in buckets, and did it only in the early hours of the day, to get maximum effect of the water, and to reduce the chance of someone thinking she was breaking the rationing rules.

Someone turned her in, anyway, when her trees in the front yard continued to do well during the heat while others in the development withered in the one-hundred-plus temperatures. Again she found Jake, Brenda, and Jayne at her walk gate one afternoon. In addition to them, there was a city water department truck parked behind Jake's Cadillac, the worker leaning against it, apart from the others.

"Now what?" Darlene asked, letting her annoyance show.

"You've been watering against the rules," Jayne said before Jake could speak.

"No, I haven't," Darlene said, keeping her voice even.

"Well, we'll just find out," Jake said and turned to the water department employee. "Read her meter."

"Sure thing, bud," said the man. His name tag read Clyde. He looked at Darlene and said. "Sorry lady. We haven't seen anything amiss in our patrols, but we have to check citizen complaints."

Darlene nodded and the man knelt down at the edge of the fence and pulled the water meter lid. After writing down the meter reading he replaced the meter housing lid and stood up.

"Well?" Jayne demanded.

"I have her records. She's used less water the last two months than she did last year when there were no restrictions." Clyde turned to look at Darlene. "Sorry, Lady. Had to check. Keep up whatever you're doing. Your lawn may be dying, but your trees sure do look good. Wish my thumb was that green."

Darlene nodded at Clyde, who was getting in his truck. She looked back at Jake, Brenda, and Jayne. "Well? I'm waiting for the apology."

Jayne stormed off without saying anything. Jake and Brenda looked sheepish, but didn't say anything. They just turned and went to Jake's car.

Realizing she was pushing her luck, Darlene started hauling water from outside the rationed area, a couple of five-gallon buckets at a time, to water the trees in the front yard. She made sure she was seen handling the buckets at the car.

She continued to add more water from the well at night, and continued to water the trees in the back yard and the garden and greenhouse from the hand pump. With the situation the way it was, Darlene let her grass grow a bit higher before she cut it, and didn't water it at all, just to keep up appearances that she was conserving water, not violating the rationing plan.

Darlene found it highly annoying that she was actually conserving more water than most, but had to hide the fact due to the petty antics of Jayne.

The price and wage controls, the precious metals recall, and all the other efforts Congress was making were not doing much to help the economy recover. Darlene was barely making it, money wise, with the small amount of temp work she was getting. But due to her well thought out preps, she was eating well enough, and making the utility payments. At least she only had to pay for what she used, utility wise, with all the blackouts, natural gas shortages, and limited water use keeping those bills down significantly from what they were before the crisis.

With August temperatures hovering between ninety-five and one-o-five, tempers rose similarly. More riots broke out. The suburbs were no long immune. Darlene's didn't have trouble until late in the month. But when it came, it was bad. Darlene lived well back in the development, and had no idea the riot was going on the next street over. The houses were well insulated.

She happened to look outside, to see if perhaps the ten percent chance of rain might be bringing in some clouds. She didn't see clouds; she saw smoke and reflected light from fires. Darlene used the telephone to call 911 to report what was going on and then hung up. She ran to her bedroom, strapped on the gun belt with the Redhawk, and threw one of the bandoleers over her left shoulder.

Picking up the Marlin 1894 she ran back to the front door. Before she could turn off the living room light the light went out. She flipped the switch down, anyway. If it was a temporary outage she didn't want to become back lighted if it came back on.

Slipping outside cautiously she wished for a moment the rifle wasn't stainless steel. It was picking up the ambient light. Darlene crouched down behind the planter to her left. The first modification Darlene had made after signing the papers for the house was to build two planter boxes, one on each side of the front door of the house.

They were tall, coming up even with the bottoms of the house windows. Rather than flowers, she had planted strawberries in them, as both a decorative plant and for the berries. She could still see out the windows, but could crouch or lie down and be behind the mass of the wide planters if someone ever took a shot at the house.

Since there was a decent slope toward the street from the house, someone would have to climb on top of a tall vehicle to get a shot over the planters into the space usually protected by them.

The second addition to the house was security shutters. They wouldn't stop high powered rifle rounds but would keep any rocks or Molotov cocktails from being thrown into the house. The circuit controlling them was on emergency power and Darlene used the security remote to close them. Darlene checked the water hose connected to a frost proof hydrant in the front wall of the house. She turned on the faucet, to fill the hoses, and laid the pistol grip nozzle handy. If needed she could spray down any fires that might be started.

The entire tract seemed to be without electricity. Darlene kept a sharp watch from her cover and saw the rioting group turn the corner and come onto her street. Flashlights waving, the rioters were throwing rocks at every house they passed. Darlene heard the sounds of glass breaking.

Then a different light flared. Someone had lighted the wick on a Molotov cocktail. A streak of flame trailed behind the jar filled with gasoline as it flew through the air toward the house three down from Darlene, on the other side of the street.

Out of the corner of her eyes Darlene caught a flash of light from Jayne and Kevin's entry porch. The two were standing in the entry watching the rioters approach, shining a flashlight toward them.

"Get back inside, you two!" Darlene whispered. Though there was no way for them to have heard her, the couple did turn and go inside. But not before the rioters had spotted the flashlight beam.

The mob's attention turned to the Noodle's house. Rocks began to fly. Unlike Darlene's gates, the Noodles had not put remote control locks on them. A dozen people opened and ran through the gates, getting close enough to really pepper the house with rocks. Windows began to shatter and Darlene was sure she heard Jayne scream.

When Darlene saw the flicker from a lighter in the process of igniting the wick of another Molotov cocktail, she raised the Marlin to her shoulder. But she was too late. The man with the jar of gasoline with a lighted wick ran through the walk gate and threw the Molotov cocktail through the Noodle's shattered living room window.

Flames immediately shot out of the window and Darlene heard Jayne scream again. Another Molotov cocktail was being readied, but not for the Noodles house. This one would be thrown at Darlene's house. The mob was moving toward her gates.

Despite the precautions she had taken, Darlene wasn't going to risk a Molotov cocktail. She stood up, the Marlin at her shoulder. "Throw that and you'll die!" she yelled at the mob. She triggered a shot into the ground at the rioter's feet. The mob began to break up and run in all directions at the sound of the shot. The man with the

Molotov cocktail tossed it just over the fence and went running with the others.

The wailing sirens of fire trucks and police cars were finally beginning to get closer. Hurriedly Darlene took off the gun belt and the bandoleer, carefully hiding them under the strawberry plants in the planter. Grabbing her garden hose, she ran out and started spraying water on the grass in the front yard that was now blazing.

She looked over and saw Kevin and Jayne standing near their front fence, watching their house go up in flames. Kevin was holding Jayne tightly, her face buried in his shoulder. Darlene felt for them, but she had her hands full with the gasoline fed grass fire.

The Noodle's house was fully involved when a fire department pumper showed up and laid lines down from the hydrant just down the street. By that time Darlene had the grass fire out and was pouring what water she could from her garden hose on the end of the Noodle's house that faced her house.

There were two reasons. One was to actually try and suppress the fire any way she could, the other was to prevent as much buildup of heat on the end of her house facing the fire. She didn't want radiant heat catching her house on fire.

Neither Kevin or Jayne came over to talk to her. They stayed by their front fence and watched the fire take their house. When the fire department had the blaze under control, Darlene went over to talk to them. "I'm so sorry," she said. "Why don't you come over to the house and sit down. It's going to be a while before the fire department finishes up."

"No, thank you," Kevin said. "We have the insurance agent coming, and a rental car is being delivered. We'll get a hotel room for now." Jayne just glared at Darlene as if the situation was her fault.

Darlene didn't argue. She went back to her yard and watched the activity. It wasn't long before the police started taking statements and the media showed up. When the officer talked to Darlene she told what she knew, leaving out the shot she had taken.

"Several people have reported a shot about the time or just after the house next door was set afire and your yard caught fire." The officer had her notebook out and was taking notes.

Darlene replied carefully. "Yes. I think so. I heard something. I think it made the guy drop the gasoline bomb just over the fence rather than try to throw it at my house."

"Do you have any idea who fired the shot? One of the tenants or a rioter?"

"I couldn't tell," Darlene said. "I'm just thankful someone did. My house might be in the same condition as the Noodles' home."

"Somehow, I don't think so," the officer replied. "You have pretty good security. Good fences, security shutters. Probably saved you rather than the gun shot."

Darlene just nodded. Suddenly thinking about Bear, she asked, "How did they get in? Bear should have been on duty. He's really careful about letting non-residents into the community."

The officer flipped back through her notebook. "That would be… Let's see… Randy Jo… Johon…"

"Johanovich. The J sounds like a Y."

"Johanovich. "Yes. He was on duty. From statements by witnesses, he was attacked while talking to a resident coming into the tract. He was beaten rather badly. Ambulance took him to County General."

"Oh my goodness! Was anyone else hurt?"

"Some glass cuts from broken windows and bruises from rocks. Thank you…" The officer checked her notes again. "Mrs. Carpenter."

"Sure. No problem. What can we do to prevent this from happening again?"

"You'll have to take that up with the current administration."

"Oh." Darlene was a bit taken aback by the officer's vehemence. Darlene went back to her entry porch and watched the activity in the area. The power was still off. She declined to comment when one of the TV news reporters called out to her.

The reporters hit a gold mine with Jayne. Darlene watched as she talked to reporter after reporter. Finally, after the fire department rolled up their hoses and departed, Darlene picked up the Marlin, bandoleer, and gun belt and went inside. After she made sure everything was locked tight, with the security shutters down, Darlene turned on the TV in the kitchen. It was on one of the emergency circuits and was receiving power from the solar electric system.

She watched the late news, switching from one to another as each had its coverage of the riot and fires. Jayne's ravings about how bad things were and their misfortune was on every station. Finally, Darlene went to bed, there being nothing else she could think of to do.

The power was still off when she got up the next morning. As she had breakfast she watched the news. The power outage had been just the one subdivision. The main transformer feeding the tract had been shot several times until it shorted out.

As more information came out, it turned out that several houses that were attacked where no one was at home were entered, easy to grab valuables taken, and the house trashed or set afire. She saw Jayne's interviews again. Finally, she turned off the TV, picked up her cell phone and dialed the County General Hospital information number, and asked about Bear.

She found out he was there, no longer in intensive care, and could have visitors. Though only a casual acquaintance through their contact at the gate to the tract, Darlene felt a kinship with him.

The hospital was some distance away, but Darlene took her bike, anyway, stopping at the only flower shop still open between her house and the hospital. A different guard was at the security kiosk. A different company entirely.

With a small plant in hand, Darlene went up to Bear's room when she found out from the emergency room where he was. It was a four-bed ward. Darlene knocked and entered the open door. The first two beds in the room had the privacy curtains closed, but the third one was open. It was Bear.

"Oh, Bear!" Darlene exclaimed softly. His face was black and blue, and swollen badly. His ribs were wrapped. He had an oxygen cannula feeding oxygen to his nostrils, and two IV bags dripping something into his left arm.

"Mrs. Carpenter. What are you doing here? Are you all right? Were you hurt last night? I tried to…"

"Hush, Bear. Don't excite yourself. I know it can't be good for you. And I'm fine. I came by to see how you were. Brought you a plant."

"You came to see me? Why?"

"Because you tried your best to protect us and paid a terrible price for it. I'm thankful you're going to be okay. You are going to be okay, aren't you?"

Bear nodded in response to the question, but said, "I didn't do a very good job of protecting you. I heard they burned several houses, and trashed more."

"Yeah. But don't worry about it, Bear. It's not your fault. You just take it easy and get well." Darlene put the potted plant on the small table beside the bed.

"I wish more people thought the way you did." Bear looked forlorn, Darlene suddenly realized.

"What? I'm sure everyone…"

"Not everyone. The Noodles are suing the security company I work for, and me personally, for what happened to them. A lawyer served the papers on me early this morning. I could lose everything I've worked so hard to get for my family. We're barely making it, as it is. I don't know how I'm going to pay the hospital bills. The company doesn't have very good insurance."

"Oh, Bear! I'm sorry. I can't imagine anyone blaming you."

"I think that's just the way they are. Always in a hurry to get through the gate, and never a word or wave of recognition. Not like you. You stop and wait patiently when I'm checking someone. Stop sometimes just to say hello."

"Surely others did the same as I?"

"Oh, there are others… were others that were nice. But most were like the Noodles, always in a hurry and not very nice, in my opinion."

"I'm sorry, Bear. I didn't know."

"Not your problem, Mrs. Carpenter. A lot of the guys have told me it's just part of the job. There are just a lot of people out there like that."

"Well, I'm glad you don't consider me one of them." A nurse came in and ushered Darlene out after that. "Get well soon, Bear," Darlene said as she left the room.

As summer turned to fall, and Darlene started getting a bit more work, she discovered that several other people, at Jayne's urging, had filed lawsuits over the riots. It turned out, that beside Bear and the security company, the Association was being sued, the security company that installed the Noodles' fire and burglary alarm, and even Stanley, as installer of the fencing, all were named in the class action suit.

She saw Jayne one time shortly after the fire, when she and Kevin were allowed to go into the house and recover a few things. Darlene stayed in her house and managed not to tell them what she thought of what they were doing.

A month later, as she was leaving for work, she saw Jayne's Mercedes and Kevin's Cadillac SUV parked at one of the few vacant houses in the tract that had never sold. There was a delivery truck parked on the street and furniture was being moved into the house.

Darlene's heart fell. She'd hoped, rather shamefully in her own eyes, that she'd seen the last of Jayne. But it appeared they were moving back into the tract. "At least not next door to me," she muttered and drove on.

The Noodles burned out shell was demolished before Christmas and the lot prepped for a new house to go up the next spring. Darlene found out after Christmas that the class action lawsuit had been settled quickly out of court.

Between the security company and the Association, something was worked out with the residents named in the suit. Darlene didn't find out the details, but it appeared that the arrangement included at least some suspended mortgage payments.

Stanley, the alarm company and Bear weren't required to pay anything, but all had some significant attorneys' fees for representation in the settlement. In Darlene's eyes, Bear was the biggest victim of the riots. Not only had he been beaten badly, racked up huge medical and attorney bills, he lost his job with the security company.

While he was recovering, and then looking for work, Darlene kept the family supplied with some food from her miniature truck garden. Frozen rabbit and fish, fresh vegetables, and even a little fresh fruit from the first of the fruit trees to start bearing. That was in addition to what she was selling at the Farmer's Market.

Darlene wouldn't sell from the house. Not only was it against CC&R's, it put her too much in the limelight. As far as she knew, no one knew about her greenhouse, well, water barrels, rear orchard, or any of the security features of the house and grounds.

Jayne and the Association knew she had a garden, but not how big, and would soon realize that the trees growing in the front yard were, in fact, fruit and nut trees, not decoratives. That was the most she wanted known. People knowing you had, when they didn't have, was just asking for trouble.

Even the sewing that she was getting was arranged at the Farmer's Market, with Darlene making deliveries. No one showed up at the house for the work, so the Association didn't know about that little business, either.

Her tax rebate from her full time work the previous year was just enough to pay the self-employment taxes she'd had working as a temp. Feeling a bit guilty about not reporting her additional income, Darlene counted up what she'd saved from the sales at the Farmers' Market. It would be enough to do another project.

While she had natural gas heat… some of the time… and the propane heaters for when the natural gas was off, she didn't have a long term solution for heat. Having done research on the Internet, Darlene knew what she wanted. And had just enough money to get it. It was another item not really addressed by the CC&R's, so Darlene decided to buy the multi-fuel outside furnace and install everything except the final connections at the furnace.

Though it could be put into action after a few minutes of work, it wasn't going to be connected and therefore couldn't be considered in use, if an issue was made of it. It turned out the unit was more expensive than her old pricing had shown, so she had to put off the installation. That would come as quickly as she got enough money together. In the meantime, the bit of money that was left, Darlene used to buy a good used chainsaw and accessories at the same place she'd picked up the rototiller.

The shop owner showed her how to use and service it, and then directed her to the National Forest office to get a wood cutting permit. Whenever she wasn't doing something else, she began cutting a Subaru load of wood and taking it home to store for when it might be needed.

As winter drew close, and the blackouts and natural gas cut-offs continued, Darlene kept saving up what she could to finish the furnace installation, except for those last connections. She was working a steady temp job, making a good wage at it, and made it through the winter in decent shape, though with the snow in the mountains, she had to give up cutting wood for a while. The Subaru was a good all weather, bad road vehicle, but it wasn't a hard core off-road vehicle, so she didn't tempt fate going where she might get stuck.

By spring, Darlene had the installation completed to the point she wanted and started saving for another project. Carrying the water for trees in the front of the house was getting annoying, but Darlene knew water was critical for their good growth. She had two options. Drive another well in the front yard and use lengths of four inch pipe she could move easily to distribute the water from the hand pump to the trees, the way she did the garden and the trees in the back yard. Or get a pump her limited electrical system could handle when the power was off.

When she was looking for pumps, she realized unlike the furnace, which had gone up, the solar pump she needed had gone down, and the small pressure pump had stayed the same price. She decided to do both projects. She waited until she had the money in the bank, and then ordered both pumps and the materials to hook them up, and the parts to drive another well, plus another hand pump.

She still wanted to maintain as low of a profile as possible. Darlene decided to camouflage the well and hand pump as a decorative water feature. As she had the first driven well, Darlene took her time, driving the well just two or three feet a day, covering the thing up with the water feature materials when she wasn't driving the well.

When she was finished, late June, she put a tapped check valve on the pipe, then a short length of pipe, and finally topped it off with the new hand pitcher pump. Small valves were attached to each of the check valve tapped openings. One was above the stopper and one below.

Rather than digging the water feature down into the ground, Darlene installed it above ground and very artistically, she thought, piled rocks around it she got for free from Stanley. She primed the pump with a bit of water, both valves turned off on the check valve. With the pump primed, Darlene filled the little pond with fresh well water.

Setting the solar powered fountain pump in the pond, she ran the waterfall hose to the top valve in the check valve and connected. She opened the valve, turned on the pump, and watched as a small stream of water began to pour from the pump spout into the pond. Those that couldn't figure it out would assume the hand pitcher pump was just as decorative as the pond water feature.

If or when she needed to use the pump, she merely had to close the top valve in the check valve, close the bottom one, and pump away. In the winter she would shut everything down, open both of the small valves so the water would drain back into the pond and well, respectively, so nothing would freeze. She had an alternate source of water for the front yard if she ever needed it.

When the other pumps came in, and Darlene had picked up a small fiberglass water tank from the farm supply store, she plumbed the two pumps and wired them up.

The solar powered pump solar panel went on the roof beside the other panels. The batteries and controller were connected and a protective box built around them in the corner of the greenhouse. The pump was connected through another tapped check valve with small valves attached, and then the outlet was connected through a tee with a valve on the side, and the hand pump was reconnected, through yet another tapped check valve. Just above the second check valve was a gate valve.

After priming the hand pump, Darlene pumped until she got water out of the hand pump and then closed the check valve. She turned on the pump and let it flow out of the valve on the tee to check it. When she knew it was working, Darlene shut the pump off and plumbed the outlet from the valve through a tee and second valve to the water tank. A float switch was added, the wires connected to the pump wiring to shut it off when the fiberglass tank was full. Off the side of the tee, a hose bib was added. The float switch had a bypass on it to override the switch so the pump could be run when the tank was full.

Darlene could fill the tank, or shut off that valve, open the hose bib, and flip the float switch bypass to run water directly from the well to where ever she wanted to run her large diameter garden hoses.

On the other end of the tank she plumbed the small Gould BF03S self-contained jet pump. The pressure tank was part of the pump body and didn't require a separate pressure tank. Darlene added a tee to the outlet, putting hose bibs in each outlet. One was connected to the house water system by running a length of garden hose with female connectors on each end to the frost proof hydrant through the wall of the house.

Darlene drew 110-volt AC power for the pump from one of the lightly loaded emergency circuits. As long as there wasn't much other load, even the solar power system would run the pump.

To get water into the house, Darlene could turn off the city water valve, open the hose bib on the pump and the frost proof hydrant. The little BF03S would kick in when the pressure dropped and draw water from the fiberglass tank. When the water level in the tank fell, the solar pump would refill it.

Rather than run down the batteries if a lot of water was needed, the generator could be started to run the Gould's pressure pump for as long as needed to water the trees in the front yard, as well as the rear garden and orchard. No more carrying water in buckets, unless she needed to do so to camouflage the fact that she had the pumps.

Darlene did like options. And she used just about every one that summer to keep the greenhouse, outside garden, both orchards, and the strawberries in the planters watered well enough for them to do well.

It was a relief not to have Jayne next door, but Jayne drove by Darlene's house arriving and leaving her new home. Every time Darlene saw her, Darlene waved, but Jayne would just lift her chin and go past, ignoring her. But a couple of times when Darlene was out of sight, but saw Jayne go by, Jayne would slow and study the place before continuing. For whatever reason, Jayne sure seemed to have it in for Darlene, if Darlene was any judge.

People seemed to have adjusted to the new way of life many of them had to lead. Cutting back to bare bones everything that could be. Selling off everything that wasn't absolutely needed, or an historical heirloom. Eating meat only every few days. Standing in lines to get a few groceries. Buying from the black market those things that couldn't be found in the legal markets.

Every state in the union and just about every major city in each of those states, plus a few smaller towns, had riots every so often. They seemed no longer protest riots, but 'grab what you can to eat or make a dollar from' looting excuses. There had not been another riot in the area of the suburbs where Darlene lived, but it would surprise no one if another occurred. They were happening regularly in other parts of the suburbs and in the city proper.

Darlene didn't know what else to do. She had cut back wherever she could, invested in things that saved money or made money, and looked for any and all work she could get. She hadn't cut her hair in months. Her shiny black hair was almost down to her waist. Facials and pedicures were out of the question, though she had really enjoyed them when Steven encouraged her to get them.

Every spare penny went into preps for the long term, because Darlene was convinced this was not a temporary situation the way some people did. She also believed it could get worse, despite many people saying 'It just can't get any worse than this!' But it did.

The US wasn't the only nation going through some trials and tribulations. The depression had spread worldwide. Many countries were even worse off than the US. And like the depression in the late twenties, early thirties of the previous century, this depression was looking like it was going to take a war to break it. And more than one country was itching to start things off.

Darlene had done everything her financial situation allowed, based on everything she'd learned on the Internet and from Stanley while she worked for him, to be ready for what she was going through, and worse.

When it happened, on a late July day, it was definitely worse, but no country actually started it.

CHAPTER THREE

-

'It' was a slow traveling, relatively small as large things of such nature go, totally unexpected, Near Earth Object, that no one knew was near Earth until two days before the sun began to break it up and the pieces started impacting earth like a gigantic shotgun blast of buck and ball.

The two days of warning probably caused as much panic and problems as would have occurred without it. People began dying literally minutes after the announcement of the pending impact came from the UN Secretary General in a world-wide broadcast at Noon, New York time. Some people with bad hearts that couldn't stand the stress of the news just keeled over.

Right on the heels of that, came killings, from simple euthanasia to hard core murder, with almost as many reasons for the killings as there were killers. Including a large number of would be killers being killed when they tried to kill someone that didn't like the idea of dying.

Darlene was working a temp job as an order picker in one of the remaining Electrical / Plumbing / HVAC warehouse operations in the area. It was going to be a pretty good placing, Darlene thought a couple of days after she'd taken the job. Since the warehouse was just about the only source of parts in the area, they were getting almost all of the existing business in the trades in the area. The pay was decent, the warehouse cool even in the worst of the summer heat, and her co-workers were a pretty good bunch.

So, when someone yelled at everyone in the warehouse to come the reception area to listen to the broadcast happening at that moment, and Darlene heard what was about to happen she said probably only the third bad word she'd ever uttered in her life.

"What do we do?" the receptionist asked.

"I'll answer that," said the General Manager of the large operation. "You keep working until we find out more."

It seemed to have the opposite effect of what the GM wanted. The room was almost empty in two minutes. Only the GM, the receptionist, and Darlene were left in the room. The GM went on a cursing streak that lasted fully a minute and a half and had words in it that Darlene had never heard; much less knew the meaning of.

Finally, he stopped, looked at Darlene and the receptionist, and said, softly. "Might as well go home until day after tomorrow. I expect you back at work when all this nonsense is over."

The receptionist almost knocked her computer keyboard off the desk in her hurry to leave.

The GM looked at Darlene. "What about you?"

"I'll wait until the panic in the streets calms down some. Last thing I want is to get run over on my bicycle by a frightened motorist trying to get home to his or her family."

"Yeah. Real or not, that's what is happening out there. You want a drink while you wait?"

Darlene shook her head and suddenly decided that maybe being out in traffic might just be better than being here with the GM now that his eyes were glinting. She turned and ran into the warehouse. Grabbing her work BOB off the Paratrooper bicycle and putting it on, Darlene then pulled her bike from the rack just inside the loading door. She looked around. The GM was just watching from the office door she'd just come through.

He just stood there as Darlene put the feet to the pedals and sped away.

It had been an easy ride to and from the warehouse the two days she'd worked there. And just like her projection of the dangers, Darlene had to be very careful not to get hit by the high speed, uncontrolled traffic on the streets.

But she made it home all right. After carefully locking the garage, Darlene went inside and turned on the TV. She happened to have commercial power at the moment. Every station that wasn't completely pre-programmed was carrying the news. Experts were hastily brought in to studios and were giving their opinion about the situation. That it was going to be a planet killer, or wouldn't have much effect except for pretty meteor showers. The opinions ran the gamut. On just about every show, since it wasn't politically correct to just stick with an opinion. Every side had to be given fair time.

Darlene watched calmly. At least outwardly so. Inside she was wracking her brain to try to figure out what else she could do to prepare for the event. If the things did hit, and she happened to be at ground zero of one of them, there wasn't much she could do to prevent or avoid it.

If one hit close, her shelter would give her some protection, but not as much as an underground one. Not enough time to do that. Probably every piece of earth moving equipment was already in use.

If a hit was at some distance, she had a good chance of surviving the impact itself. The aftermath wasn't a sure thing.

If any and all impacts were well away from her, the odds went up for surviving the event, as did surviving the early post impact timeframe. Long term… She was as ready as she had been able to provide for.

Thoughts of going to get a 'few more things' crossed her mind, but she weighed the pros and cons and the cons won out. Too big a risk for too small a reward. Best to batten down the hatches immediately and go with the flow, no matter what happened.

Darlene got up, did a couple loads of laundry that needed doing, made herself a bit of lunch, worked in the garden, orchards, and greenhouse, and then checked the TV again. Same ol' same ol'.

A good supper, long bath, and one last check of the TV before going to bed. At least there was consensus that there would be no impacts before approximately five in the evening the following day, New York time. The initial impacts, if there were any, would be on the dark side of the world.

Darlene went to bed, and surprisingly, fell right to sleep.

She was up early the next morning and checked the news again. The opinions weren't quite as wide spread. Yes, there would be impacts, but they would all be small. No, the planet wouldn't be destroyed completely, but human kind still might perish.

Darlene spent the day tidying up things, especially outdoors. She didn't want anything blowing away if she could help it. She readied the shelter, though there wasn't that much to be done.

By five New York time, like billions of others that had a TV, Darlene was in front of it, to see what could be seen, if anything.

"There was something," the particular on-camera newswoman said, pointing up into the dark sky of central China. "There! There's another!"

The screen went white for a moment, and then another news reader came on, also out in the open, pointing at the many streaks showing up in the sky.

Another white screen and the anchor man came on. He was in the network's offices. "I'm sorry, Ladies and

Gentlemen. We seem to be losing contact with our crews as the earth turns into this onslaught of extraterrestrial material slowly but surely. We hope to have…"

The screen went white and then black. When nothing happened for several seconds, Darlene tried another channel. It went black almost immediately. Communications were failing faster than she could switch channels. Finally, she just turned the TV off, looked at her watch, and then went outside into the twilight that would soon be full dark.

Darlene checked her fence gates. Locked tight. She triggered the security remote and the security shutters on the doors and windows began to close, except for the walkway door into the garage from the driveway. Taking the lawn chair, she'd left out when putting things away earlier, she put it on the driveway where she could look east.

Sipping from a glass of iced tea, she talked to a couple of the neighbors that had come outside themselves and saw her sitting there.

"How can you just sit there?" asked Mandy Benson. She was Darlene's west side neighbor. They knew one another enough to carry on a conversation, but that was about it. The only real dealings Darlene had had with

Mandy and Archibald Benson was about the fences, such a long time ago, it seemed like now.

"Nothing I can do," Darlene said with a shrug. "We get hit or we don't."

There was a long period of silence as more and more people came out to watch for the impending impacts. Assuming there would be some. For some reason the majority of those people close came over to stand around Darlene's driveway gate.

"How long are you going to wait?" someone asked, directing the question to Darlene. It was someone she didn't know from down the block.

"Just until I see one in the sky, or see an impact." The words were barely out of Darlene's mouth when the eastern skyline lit up. "Like that," Darlene added. "I'm going inside. I suggest the rest of you do, too."

Calmly Darlene got up, folded the chair, picked up the iced tea from the driveway, and turned to the garage. The others erupted into panic as one streak of light zoomed over their heads with a screaming sound.

Darlene opened the door into the garage, closed the security door after she closed the regular door, set the chair aside, and went into the shelter, locking the two heavy wood and steel doors behind her. One at the outside entrance and the other at the entrance from the baffled entry hall. She was sealed in.

With only one battery powered LED light glowing, Darlene went to her knees, looked up at the ceiling of the shelter, brought her hands together, and then began to pray, her words barely audible.

The long prayer done, Darlene got into one of the four bunks in the shelter and laid down, wrapping herself in the blanket that was on the bunk. She turned to face the wall and waited, eyes closed, for whatever might come.

Darlene felt the shelter shake many times, one time violently. After what seemed an eternity, but was actually only three hours, the shocks stopped.

She tried one of the security cameras that had a feed into the shelter. It faced the street in front of the house, and several houses across the street from her. Everything looked fine, except for it being very dark, even at night. The commercial power was off again. She tried a camera that pointed east. She could see more of the sky. Such as it was. Just one ugly blackness all the way to the horizon. She could see the reflections of flames on the bottom of the dust cloud.

Checking the remote reading radiation meter, Darlene discovered that there was only background radiation. Then she looked at the weather panel. At first she thought everything was normal, but when the display changed to outside temperature she gasped. It was almost one hundred and fifty degrees outside, while still only seventy-one inside.

Determined to stay inside until the temperature came down, Darlene fixed another glass of iced tea, and sat down at the counter that held the computer, radios, weather instrument, and inside air quality monitors.

The CO_2 level was still within limits but rising slowly. She didn't have a headache yet. Opening up the laptop computer, Darlene did some reading of the various prep information she'd gathered from the internet and boned up on CO_2.

It would be some time before she needed to hang CO_2 adsorption blankets, and more time than that before adding oxygen from the bottles stashed between the back wall of the shelter and the garage wall. The adsorption blankets and oxygen equipment had been the hardest items to get for the shelter, and the most expensive items. Though she'd had to fudge the truth a little, and eat light for a couple of months, she'd managed to get them.

When the CO_2 alarm sounded, Darlene was starting to get a headache. She put up the curtains and waited for the CO_2 to drop. It did, slowly, but steadily. The oxygen level was down, but still adequate. The humidity was up so Darlene turned on the small de-humidifier in the shelter. The temperature inside the shelter was up to seventy-three degrees. Outside temperature down ten degrees to one forty.

Over the next couple of days Darlene napped for a while when she added oxygen to the shelter or hung fresh adsorption blankets, as it gave her time to get some real sleep without worrying about the shelter environment for a few hours.

She didn't even think about going outside until the outside temperature was down below one hundred twenty. When it had fallen that low, Darlene transferred the various atmospheric sensors to an isolation cabinet she'd made from an acrylic fish tank and a few parts from Radio Shack.

Opening a small valve, Darlene turned on the small fan that drew air from outside, through the isolation tank, and back outside. The sensor changed readings slightly, but, to Darlene's great relief, oxygen, CO_2, and carbon monoxide were within safe limits.

Still, when she stripped down and put on a lightweight Tyvek coverall with attached booties and hood, Darlene donned a respirator, too. Hesitating only a moment, Darlene wrapped the gun belt with the holstered Redhawk around her waist and buckled it in place. There had been no indications of hard radiation, but she made sure she had her pocket alarm in her pocket before she went outside.

Hesitating a moment, Darlene then opened the sealed door to the entry hall, and locked and sealed it behind her. Next she opened the door into the garage. She stopped there and looked around in the light from the bright six D-cell Maglite flashlight. So far, so good. A few things had been jostled about by the ground shocks, but nothing critical was damaged.

Crossing her fingers, Darlene tried the security door remote. The walk through door shutter began to open. "Yes!" Darlene said. There was still power in the battery bank for the house. There were some dead fish, and the water level was low in the fish tank.

Darlene stepped out into the faint light and looked around. There was enough light to see so she slipped the flashlight into a deep pocket in the coveralls. She made a circle around the house. Only on the east side did anything look amiss. The wall of the house and the roof looked different, somehow, and the trees in the orchard had shriveled leaves on their east facing sides.

The rabbits were dead in their hutches. There didn't seem to be many worms, but there were some.

Next Darlene went out into the street and began to check neighbors' houses. She stopped after the sixth house full of bodies. There had been a couple of bodies out on lawns and in the street, but their faces were so badly blistered from the flash that must have occurred, and the heat afterwards, she couldn't tell who they were, even if she might have known them.

Lightning began to flash and Darlene felt a hot breeze. It looked like it would storm.

Turning around, Darlene went back to the garage. After taking out the dead fish and taking them out to the garden spot, she drained the tank down until the remaining fish were flapping around in an inch or so of water. Darlene activated the well pump and refilled the fish tank.

Just be before she went into the shelter, Darlene lifted the respirator and took a deep breath. The air smelled of char and heat and dead fish, and was hot in her lungs, but she didn't pass out or feel ill. She took another breath just to be sure and then went in; sealing the doors behind her again, ready to take some pure oxygen to flush her lungs if she did react.

She monitored herself for several long minutes, but felt no ill effects from having breathed the outside air. Then, bathed in sweat from the heat outside, she stripped off the coverall and stepped into the shower in the small bathroom in one corner of the shelter.

Refreshed, Darlene fixed a bite to eat, checked the air in the shelter again, and laid down for a nap. That heat had just sucked the strength out of her.

When she woke, Darlene began scanning the Amateur Radio bands. Nothing but static at the moment. With as much particulate matter as was obviously in the air and the possibility of electrical phenomena in the turbulent atmosphere, such as the heavy lightning, she really wasn't expecting anything for several more days.

She slipped into a routine similar to that she'd followed before going outside. Before she explored further she wanted the outside temperature to come down more, and hopefully some of the dust to drift out of the atmosphere. She would still need a dust mask and goggles, but hopefully she wouldn't need the respirator.

Keeping an eye on the outside by the cameras and monitor, Darlene saw the sky lighten just a bit every day, with light to heavy rain coming every day or so. It was washing some of the atmospheric contamination out of the sky, but Darlene decided it would be years, if not decades, before it all back down on the ground. Darlene said a little prayer to ask that there be enough sunlight for gardens to grow.

Nine days after the fact, with the temperature outside a bearable ninety-five degrees, Darlene dressed for the heat, armed herself, and went to check more of the housing tract. She'd tried the car and it had started right up, but she didn't want to use it yet. Partly because of the dust, but also because she could see and go places on her bike she couldn't if in the car.

There was enough light to see, and Darlene could easily tell where the sun was, but things were a long way from normal.

The bodies she found were highly desiccated. The extreme heat had dried them out before they could begin to decompose. Even those that had died inside were mummified, for the most part.

It took her three days to check every house in the tract that she could get into. If the place was locked up tight she left it as it was. Only those houses that had at least one door unlocked would she enter. She kept a log of what she found, including bodies. Something would have to be done about them, but there was no way she could handle it on her own.

It was eerie riding the bicycle around. It was almost totally silent. No birdsongs, traffic sounds, insects chirping. Nothing. Except for the thunder. That came often, often loud enough to hurt Darlene's ears. Whenever she heard thunder, even if she didn't see lightning first, she found overhead shelter. The lightning was horrific and the thunder just as bad. The rains came down in sheets, hot and muddy still.

Darlene finally took the Subaru out of the garage and left the tract to see what might lie outside of it. More of the same, mostly, she discovered. And then she found the first survivor besides herself.

It was a young woman and when she saw the Subaru she ran into the large C-store she'd been standing in front of. Darlene pulled into the parking lot and stopped. When she got out the Redhawk was in the holster on her belt, and she gripped the Marlin in her right hand.

"Hello!" Darlene called, opening the door a fraction. "Hello! Are you there? I'm not going to hurt you. Come on out!"

"Are you a girl?" came a quivering voice.

"Yes, I am," Darlene answered, opening the door a bit more.

"Are there any guys with you? I won't come out if there are any guys with you."

"No. I'm alone. Are you all right?"

Slowly the woman stepped around the corner of the stores walk-in cooler. When she didn't see anyone besides Darlene she ran forward and hugged Darlene before Darlene could react.

"Hey! Hey! It's okay. You're all right now. What happened here? How did you survive? What's your name?"

"Milly." That was all for a few moments. Then Milly stepped away from Darlene and took a look out the door of the store.

"You really alone?"

"I am. Can you tell me what's been going on? How did you survive?"

"I was on late shift. I saw the things in the sky. And then it got even darker than night and really hot. I got in the walk-in cooler with a couple of the customers. But they didn't stay. They talked about it and said they were going to make a run for it. I never saw them again.

"I just stayed in the cooler, drinking the drinks and water and eating the sandwiches." Her nose turned up for a moment. "The toilet wouldn't work and I used one of the plastic buckets from the fast food part of the store to go to the bathroom. It stinks."

Milly seemed calmer, but she suddenly tensed. "Two days ago I was out looking around. Two guys chased me, but I got away and hid. They just kept looking and looking and looking and telling me what they were going to do to me when they caught me. They're still around here somewhere. That's why I hid when I saw you."

"We are for a fact, still around," came a voice from behind Darlene. "And there are two now, Harry. We each get one."

"Yeah. And then the other one." Both men laughed.

Darlene didn't hesitate. She knew she couldn't afford to. Survivors like these two would make living in the new world untenable. Moving quickly and fluidly, Darlene spun around, raising the Marlin to her shoulder at the same time. As soon as the front sight touched human form she fired and worked the lever, and continued to swing the gun in an arc.

She heard a shot that wasn't her gun, and then her sights were crossing over another human form. Again she fired. The first man had gone down immediately. This second one, hit in the shoulder was able to fire his pistol again.

Darlene felt a burning sensation on her left leg, but had worked the lever of the Marlin again automatically and drew another bead. That heavy .44 Magnum hollow point slug took the top of the man's head off from the nose up.

Darlene didn't realize Milly was screaming and screaming again until the action was over. She went over to Milly and put her arm over her shoulders, turning her away from the carnage of the two men. The first man had taken the hollow point at the base of his throat, into the spine, half decapitating him.

"Milly," Darlene said, "Wait right here. I need to check them."

"Are they dead?" asked Milly, keeping her face toward the front door.

"Oh, yeah. They're dead. These were the two after you?"

"Un-huh."

Darlene picked up both pistols, and then checked the bodies for magazines. Both had two for their respective weapons. The first one had a wicked looking Spyderco

CO8 Harpy hawk bill serrated folding blade knife. The second had a more conventional knife, but it was razor sharp. She wiped the blood off the things on the shooter's pants and then went back to join Milly.

"Milly, do you know if any of your family survived?"

"I don't know. I've been afraid to leave here in case it gets hot again. It was so hot I could barely stand it."

Darlene looked back at the two dead men. Both their faces and hands were badly blistered. How they suffered that and survived for as long as they did, Darlene wasn't sure.

"Come on. You're going with me," Darlene told Milly and headed out the door.

"Will you take me home?"

"I will. We'll see if your family is okay. If they aren't, don't worry, you can stay with me."

A subdued Milly followed Darlene out to the Subaru. She gave directions to Darlene on how to get to her house. Milly, like Darlene, wasn't holding out much hope for her family, and it showed when they got there. "Will you look?" Milly asked Darlene.

"Okay. You sit here and I'll check." The front door of the house was unlocked and Darlene went inside. It was the same as so many others. People in poses of trying get away from the heat. In the tub, presumably with running water at the time. In front of the open doors of refrigerators and freezers.

Darlene stripped blankets and sheets off a couple of the beds and covered the bodies. She went outside and called to Milly. "Milly, I've covered the bodies. I want you to come in and get some clothes and things to bring with you to my place."

It was like a recalcitrant child delaying going to school to get Milly in the house. When she did go inside, she grabbed things as quickly as she could and ran back out to the Subaru, clutching everything in her arms to her chest. Darlene looked for and found a suitcase. She took it outside and helped Milly get her things inside, and then close the case.

Darlene decided she'd done enough for the day and drove home, not seeing another soul.

Milly didn't even question the fact that Darlene had electricity and running water. She just took advantage of them to bathe and change clothes, then eat the meal Darlene prepared. Darlene set her up in one of the bedrooms and suggested she get some sleep.

"It's so hot!" Milly complained when she went into the bedroom.

"Yes, I guess it is," Darlene said. She'd been sleeping in the shelter, since it was several degrees cooler, and she felt secure there. She wasn't quite ready to let Milly know about it.

"Come on into the living room. It has a ceiling fan. You can sleep on the sofa under it."

Milly eagerly followed and Darlene turned the fan on. It was probably as much psychological, as the fan merely stirred the eighty-five-degree air.

When it was full dark again, Darlene closed all the security shutters and prepared for bed herself, luxuriating under the cool shower spray for several minutes.

Darlene was up at her normal time the next morning and opened up the house. It was still hot, but the temperature had dropped another three degrees, to eighty-two degrees. She prepared a breakfast, but Milly was still sleeping soundly. Darlene didn't have the heart to wake her, trying to imagine the terror the young woman had endured those many days alone in the C-store's cooler, and then hiding from the two men.

Suddenly Darlene was wondering why she didn't feel bad about having taken two lives. Especially now, when the population of earth may have fallen by ninety-percent or more. "But scum is scum, no matter how many people are living or dead," she said to the window as she looked out on the back yard.

When Milly began to scream, Darlene ran into the living room and took the frightened girl into her arms. "Easy, Milly. You're okay. You're safe with me."

It took a couple of minutes, but Milly calmed down and then hurriedly went to the bathroom, after looking around the room and getting her bearings. Darlene went back into the kitchen and Milly followed a few minutes later, still in her pajamas.

After warming up Milly's breakfast she gave her the plate and watched as she fiddled with the food, eating very little of it.

"Milly," Darlene said when Milly pushed the plate back and stretched, "You need to finish that up. We don't have food to spare and can't afford to waste any. And you'll need your strength to…"

"You're not my mother! You can't tell me what to do. I'm an adult." Milly reached over and flipped the plate off the counter, staring at Darlene.

Darlene held her temper and cleaned up the mess before she spoke. "Milly, if you expect to live under my roof, you will follow my rules."

"Fine. Didn't ask for help and don't need help. I'll take my stuff and get out of your hair, you mean old woman!"

"Milly, don't be like…"

Milly wasn't listening she stomped out of the kitchen and went to the room Darlene had intended her sleep in. Five minutes later she came out, carrying the suitcase. "Give me some food!" she demanded. "I'm leaving."

"Well, young lady, if you want to leave you may do so, but I'm not wasting any of my food on you. There's plenty out there for the taking, if the heat hasn't ruined it."

Darlene didn't know what to do. She didn't want Milly out on her own. If the first contacts were any indication, the post-apocalyptic world was going to be a dangerous place in which to live. But there was no way Milly was going to act like a spoiled thirteen-year-old in Darlene's house. She was an adult and needed to act like one.

After those few minutes of thought, Darlene went to the front door and looked out to see if Milly might not just be trying to worry her, by pretending to leave.

"Nope," Darlene said. She saw Milly across the street trying to get the neighbor's car started. Darlene just watched. Finally, Milly had the car started, backed out of the driveway and took off, screeching the tires when she floored the accelerator. The engine was running rough at first, but Darlene heard it settle down before Milly made the corner. Milly took the first corner on two wheels, and Darlene heard more squealing tires as Milly made her way out of the subdivision.

Hurt and annoyed both, Darlene wiped away tears that had started to roll down her cheeks. "It is her life. She's entitled to do what she wants with it."

A moment later Darlene straightened up and said, "Quit feeling sorry for yourself! Time to go do some more exploring. If Milly survived, there are almost certainly others in the area."

There were, but it took Darlene several days to find them. There were individuals here and there, and a couple of families that had made it. All had similar experiences and had suffered much more than Darlene had in her shelter. Deep basements, bank vaults, walk in coolers like

Milly used… All given just enough protection to save lives, but the survivors had all suffered terribly from the heat.

Many were desperate for water and Darlene began hitting every little and large store she passed to pick up bottles of water and easily digested foods, such as simple soups. Until the survivors she found had recuperated enough to fend for themselves, Darlene made a regular round checking on them and handing out the food she got at stores.

Finally, after a month, those that Darlene had found and helped began helping themselves. Then Darlene decided to check the hospital. She'd thought of it several times before, but had put it out of her mind. It was going to be a bad situation, and Darlene knew it.

But she went, and discovered a group of survivors at the hospital numbering more than the total of individuals and family she'd already found. A total of fifty-four had survived in the deep basement shelter of the hospital. And they weren't all patients and staff of the hospital. It was some time before Darlene found out the details, but when she saw Kevin and Jayne Noodles she had an uneasy feeling that things had not been pleasant or easy.

At least the group was organized, to a degree. Thanks to one Dr. Brian James, who had simply taken charge and run the shelter. But there was only a degree of cooperation. There were many that had disagreed with Dr. James and made their disagreement known often and loudly, Darlene discovered.

There were essentially three groups at the hospital. The largest being the one Dr. James led with most of the staff of the hospital and the few patients that had survived willingly following.

The second was a small group, apparently with no real leader, but including Kevin and Jayne, that had caused all sorts of trouble for the Doctor from the time they arrived and demanded entry till the time Darlene showed up.

The third group was about a third of the total group. They were leaderless as well, and tended to back, as a group, first the Doctor, and then the malcontents, as each subject came up for debate.

Forays had been taken in the area around the hospital and food and water obtained, but everyone was still staying at the hospital, many in the shelter, with only a small handful of Dr. James' group doing the foraging and gathering of supplies for the others.

They also were responsible for clearing the dead from the hospital and burying them. A construction project nearby had a backhoe that one of the men could operate, so the burial wasn't that difficult. Just heart rending.

As soon as Jayne saw Darlene, with her skin still as smooth and untouched as before the impacts, she became almost hysterical. Jayne's once beautiful skin was as red and blistered as the rest of those that had endured the one-hundred-forty-degree heat in the shelter during the worst of the heat outside. Unlike Darlene's sealed shelter, the hospital shelter had to bring in outside air, even when it was the hottest, to breathe.

Dr. James came over and, with Kevin's help, got Jayne calmed down. It took a Valium to get Jayne to calm down and shut up.

"You know her?" Dr. James asked Darlene when he walked over to her after dealing with Jayne. Darlene had made herself scarce, to lessen the stress on Jayne while the Doctor was talking to her.

"We used to be next-door neighbors," Darlene replied. "We still live in the same subdivision, but not next door to each other."

"That's probably a good thing," said the Doctor with a chuckle. "She seems to think you caused all this trouble."

"I'm not surprised," Darlene said, a wry smile curving her lips. "She's hasn't liked me from the day I moved in. It had been her best friend's house before I moved in. She blamed me for her leaving, too."

"I see. And may I ask how you have managed to survive, with so little physical ailments?"

"I have a shelter at my house," Darlene said, having immediately trusted Dr. James after talking to him upon her arrival. "Sealed myself in. The temperature inside never got above eighty."

"But CO_2?"

"I had adsorption material and medical oxygen to supplement the original air content of the shelter."

"Wow. You sound like you were expecting this."

"Not this specifically, though it was one of the things I considered when I built the shelter."

"So. Are you one of those survivalists out to overthrow the government? Kind of a moot point now, I'd venture to say."

The Doctor noted the annoyance in Darlene's face. "I was not, and am not, one of those 'Survivalists' you hear… heard about in the media before all this. I prepared for hard times, not the overthrow of the government. I don't plan to start my own country. Or church, for that matter."

"Sore spot, I take it." The Doctor was smiling.

"Yeah. I guess so."

"So. You know how to survive. What do you suggest we do?"

"Oh, no! I'm not getting involved in this group. I've got my hands full trying to get the other survivors I've found to deal with things on their own."

Dr. James was surprised. "You mean there are others, besides those of us in the hospital?"

"Yes. Didn't you know?"

Dr. James shook his head. "I just assumed we were the only ones, and we barely made it at that."

"Others had basements. There was one family stayed in a bank vault. And several people took up residence in store walk-in coolers."

"Oh. I see. So we really need to get organized, with this many people to see to, and no help coming."

"Don't really know if there will be any help," Darlene said slowly. "I haven't been able to raise anyone on Amateur Radio. If we survived, I'm sure there are others. Some areas probably weren't nearly as badly affected as we were." There was a pause and then Darlene added. "Of course, there are bound to be huge areas where no one survived."

"That, I'm sure of. Now, what should we do?"

Darlene sighed. "The basics. I imagine the sewer will stop up, if it hasn't already. Need to dig temporary latrines. Send out salvage parties to keep supplied with food and water. You have medical supplies, I would think."

Dr. James smiled and nodded.

"But all of you can't stay here. There are countless houses in the area that are vacant. Or will be when the bodies are removed and buried. I suggest people take up residence in homes near useable water supplies, plant gardens, and salvage everything edible in the entire area of operations. The homes need to have fireplaces or wood stoves, and teams shou…"

"Fireplaces and wood stoves? In this heat?"

"This won't last. I don't know when it will happen, but sometime in the mid-term to long-term future, all the debris in the air is going to trigger a swing to colder temperatures. Perhaps even an ice age."

"I thought it would stay hot. Greenhouse gasses and all."

"It might. That's one theory. I happen to believe the lack of sunlight will have a bigger impact than the extra greenhouse gases produced."

"I see."

"And…" Darlene said, a bit reluctantly, "You might want to think about arming some of the people. I've already run into survivors that aren't playing by societies rules."

"Yeah. I noticed the pistol you carry."

"It's a double action revolver, not a pistol. But that's beside the point. Yes. I do. And I intend to keep carrying it all the time, for the foreseeable future. I'll not have survived this event to be taken or killed by someone that thinks there are no more rules and they can do anything they please without worrying about consequences."

"You are quite adamant about this," the Doctor said, studying Darlene's face.

"I am. Anyone that doesn't like it can just stay away from me." She looked the Doctor right in the eyes when she said it.

He nodded. "I understand. Don't really approve, but you are too valuable a resource to run off."

"Now look! I am not a resource for you! You have plenty of people to take care of business. I suggest you go about doing it."

"Sorry. Didn't mean to make you angry. Look. You've already given advice worth its weight in gold. Just try to keep in contact. I think all the survivors in this area are going to have to get along and cooperate if any of us are to survive very long."

Somewhat mollified, Darlene nodded. "I'll keep in touch. And leave you with one warning. Look out for Jayne Noodles. She's trouble."

"Funny. That's one of the things she said about you."

"I bet. Probably the mildest thing she said."

"It was, actually."

"I'll try to get by every few days to see how you're doing here." She held out her hand and the Doctor shook it.

"Thank you for doing what you are," he said, and then turned when someone called his name.

Darlene made an unobtrusive exit, her mind full of possibilities and potential problems. She was seeing more problems that positive possibilities. With what she'd learned in the past hour or so, Darlene made it a point to stop at the first store she came to and filled the rear of the

Subaru with foods suitable for long term storage, and many other items of use for long term survival. For herself.

The slightly haphazard way she'd been gathering things for others had to come to an end. Salvage must be planned and carried out carefully. But she wasn't going to disadvantage herself totally for the sake of others.

On the way home Darlene stopped at the big park that lay between her subdivision and the next. It had a large lake. Darlene was relieved to see that, though the high heat had evaporated significant amounts of the water, the rains had replenished it somewhat from the last time she'd checked.

Darlene did a great deal of thinking that evening, late into the night. Of course she would help, where she could, but she wasn't going to give up her independence to take care of people that had made no preparations for anything, much less the event they were in the process of surviving.

CHAPTER FOUR

-

Well aware that processed foods would eventually run out, Darlene included rabbits and chickens in her search for long term supplies. She decided to go to the place where she'd bought her first set of breeder rabbits.

It was a gruesome sight. Most of the rabbits were dead in their hutches. But Darlene found several, rather skinny, rabbits running loose around the place. The only thing she could figure was that the owner had turned loose several to fend for themselves. Probably his favorites.

The rabbits were all docile and Darlene didn't have much trouble picking them up and putting them in cages she found stacked by the hutches. She gave all of them water and some feed, which they devoured with relish. Darlene loaded all the rabbit feed and as well as all of the paraphernalia the dead owner had to raise rabbits on a large scale that she didn't already have.

It took her a week of looking in the area to find any live chickens. She wasn't sure how they had survived the event, but they obviously had. Then she spotted the open crawlspace under the two-story house. When she approached that was where the chickens bolted to. Apparently the crawlspace had been adequate shelter for at least some of the chickens. Not all had survived, as there were dead chickens here and there on the property.

Darlene blocked the entrance to the crawlspace and then looked around the small farm. Everything she would need to capture and carry the chickens was there. She left as the light faded. She got the rabbits she'd found in her hutches, ate a light supper, secured the house, and went to bed.

She was up before daylight the next day and on the way to get the chickens. It was light when she arrived. It took an hour to rig an enclosed pen at the crawlspace opening. When it was done, Darlene donned one of her Tyvek coveralls, added a dust mask and goggles, grabbed the Maglite six D-cell flashlight, and wiggled under the house. She turned and adjusted the head for a tight light.

It took four times as long as she expected, and she wound up losing three of the birds, but when she finished up, Darlene had two roosters, seventeen hens, and a good thirty chicks. It was deafening in the Subaru on the way back home. With the chickens in their new home, Darlene went back and stripped the small farm of its chicken raising equipment, and all the feed and supplements she could find.

It took her a week to get the rear of the Subaru cleaned thoroughly enough to eliminate the chicken smell. But she was again well fixed for small stock meat production, as well as eggs.

The temperatures had continued to drop, reaching normal for the area several weeks after the impacts. Darlene finally made contact with several Amateur Radio Operators using her unlicensed equipment. There were many survivors, spread out all around the world, though she made only one contact in the areas of Russia, China, and all of Africa. It seems that area took a second round of hits twenty-four hours after the first impacts.

Eastern Europe had been hit with the second round, too, but there were only a handful of additional hits in Western Europe and the Atlantic Ocean.

Australia had been peppered, but with the low population density, there were a higher percentage of survivors.

All-in-all, North, Central, and South America had fared fairly well, if eight-five percent loss of life instead of ninety-five percent could even be called that.

But the information told Darlene what she was desperate to know. There wouldn't be any help coming from outside the US. It and every other nation were going to be on its own for a very long time.

Between dozens of impact generated tsunamis in every ocean, and enough heat generated by the impacts to melt Northern Hemisphere land locked ice and most of the ice on Antarctica, coastlines around the world had changed. Entire coastal cities and populations had been wiped off the face of the world. The world's oceans were almost forty feet higher than normal already, and rising. But that was about to change.

With the fresh water influx to the North Atlantic, the Gulf Stream sank. And the temperature didn't stop dropping when it reached normal in any part of the world. It should have stayed in the high seventies where Darlene was. But the thermometer kept dropping a degree or so every few days as the tremendous rains continued on a nearly daily basis.

Darlene was never quite sure why the exodus from the hospital ended up in her little domain, when it happened. Perhaps it was because that is where Jayne and Kevin lived. They essentially led the way. Darlene didn't think the Noodles were any happier about it than she was.

But people began filtering in, taking up residence in the vacant homes. Even many of those survivors that Darlene had found individually got the word and moved in. Most just stacked the bodies from their new homes two or three houses down, if it was empty. When she saw it, Darlene immediately found Dr. James. It wasn't hard. He'd taken the house next to Darlene.

"We have to do something about the bodies," she told him.

Dr. James rubbed his forehead. "I know. I told the people that, but no one wants to do it."

The two were standing by Dr. James walk gate. When a voice came from behind Darlene she jumped and her hand went to the Redhawk revolver on her hip.

"Geez! Bear! Don't do that!" she exclaimed when she turned around and saw who it was. Bear and his family had managed to survive on their own. Like

Darlene, Bear had a good shelter. But it didn't include the air monitoring and handling options Darlene's did. He and the family had suffered from the heat as much as the others, despite being well prepared.

"I'll do it," Bear said. "I can run a backhoe. We just have to find one around here."

"There's one at the hospital," Dr. James said.

Almost as one voice, Darlene and Bear each said, "That's too far." Darlene continued. "Can't afford to waste the fuel. There won't be any new fuel for a long time. At least, not in this area."

"She's right. There's bound to be something close," Bear added.

"I'll go looking. Even as desiccated as they are, we don't want the bodies out in the open. Eventually dogs and other animals that survived will start feeding on them. That's just not a good thing, any way you look at it."

With her own words in her mind, Darlene took the Paratrooper bicycle on the search. She picked an area that she hadn't already been through, knowing there were no construction projects going on it those areas.

It didn't take as long as she thought it would. A mile and a half toward the edge of town a new mall was going in. There was any type of equipment they might need. After getting back to her house she took the Subaru out of the garage and went to get Bear. He and his family had taken the house the other side of the Noodles old lot.

Darlene took it upon herself to make the decision to bury the dead at the mall building site. It would use fewer resources to move the bodies that far than moving the backhoe. Plus, there wasn't a really good place within the development to bury them. There'd already been objections to the plan on that basis.

So Bear began to dig the hole and Darlene went to find volunteers to move the bodies. She didn't have much luck. It came down to her and Dr. James. With Bear's help they got one of the dump trucks at the construction site started and the two used it to move the bodies.

Darlene loaned the Doctor a facemask and a pair of leather gloves. Equipped the same way, the nasty work commenced. There could be no gentleness to it, with just the two of them working. They had to swing the bodies back and forth a couple of times to get the momentum to toss them up to the front of the dump truck body.

Dr. James and Darlene were thankful for the cooler temperatures. They didn't stop when the regular afternoon rain came. Darlene shivered once, but put it off to the strain of handling the bodies.

It took three full days to get all the bodies inside the walled development moved and buried. That included quite a few animal carcasses in addition to the human. It was all Darlene could do to make herself handle the several babies and toddlers that had perished. Those got special handling. They were set gently down in the dump truck right at the rear, and then laid carefully down in the mass grave.

Darlene kept to herself for several days after that. But the needs of the community intruded again, bringing her out of the doldrums handling the bodies had caused. Dr. James was ringing the walk gate buzzer and Darlene went out to meet him.

"Now what?" she asked, seeing the sheepish look on the Doctor's face. "More problems?"

Dr. James nodded. "People are telling me the sewer is backing up. Most people are hauling water from the lake and flushing toilets with it, but they're backed up now."

"Well, for goodness sake! I told you they needed to dig latrines or build outhouses! Without commercial power the sewer system won't work!"

"Some of them just don't want to do that. They want power back and sewer."

"Not going to happen. At least, not for a long time. We might eventually get septic tanks and drainage fields put in for everyone, but that'll take months and a lot of cooperation."

"I'll tell them it's backyard outhouses for now. Uh… What do you think about getting the water turned back on?"

"Crimeny, Doc! Don't you listen? No electricity, no water! Until we can find someone to put in a local well, and get a pump and tank, and a generator to run it… It's hauling from the lake, or drive your own."

"Drive your own?" Dr. James' brow was furrowed in confusion.

Darlene winced. She shouldn't have let that slip. "Well, if they can find the parts, the water table isn't that far down, and they can drive a well. It's what I did."

She let Dr. James through the gate and walked over to the water feature just off the walkway.

"That's just a fountain, isn't it?"

Darlene shook her head. "I did that so no one would bother me about it. It's only an inch and a quarter well. It would handle one house, but that's all. The lake is still the best source of water. Though… rather than boil it for drinking water…" She gave Dr. James a sharp look. "People are boiling the water from the lake, aren't they?"

"Well… They're supposed to be. I've had a couple of cases of bad diarrhea that might be caused by bad water."

Darlene looked down at the ground for a long moment. "Okay. This water is good. I had it tested and I don't think the impacts would have changed that. Anyone that wants clean drinking water can come get it." She frowned at the Doctor. "But only at certain times of the day. I'm not going to have people in the yard messing around when I'm not here or at all hours of the day when I am here.

"You tell them they have to provide their own containers and fill them between six AM and seven AM in the morning, and six and seven in the evening. If I'm not here some of those times, they'll just have to wait until I am here."

"That seems reasonable."

"Don't bet on some of the others thinking that."

Darlene was right. People started showing up as soon as word got around. Darlene went ahead and let those with containers fill them, but refused to turn loose any of her garden buckets for anyone to use.

Then Kevin and Jayne showed up. "I knew you were doing something against the CC&R's," Jayne said. She stopped outside the fence and motioned at Kevin. "Give her the jugs. We'd better not get sick because of this water," Jayne added.

Darlene had made no move to come over to the fence to get the milk jugs from Kevin. "You'll have to pump it yourself."

"Figures!" Jayne hissed. "Do it, Kevin."

A quiet and obedient Kevin did that when Darlene used the remote to unlock the gate. As it was, Darlene wound up holding the jugs in place for Kevin to use the pump to fill them. He couldn't do both.

"From now on, it's six to seven, morning and evening," Darlene said as Kevin went back through the gate.

"You haven't changed since all this, have you?" Jayne asked. "Still the superior little witch that wants to make her own rules and have everybody else live by them. Even carry a gun to make sure everyone follows along."

Darlene was livid, but she stayed where she was and swallowed the angry comment she was about to make. "Think what you want, Jayne. You always do."

Chin up; Jayne stalked off, Kevin following docilely. Darlene went into the house to cool down, muttering to herself as she went.

Not much of Darlene's garden had survived the days of high heat. She was using the tiller on it to mix in the remains when she heard the bell ring that she'd fastened to the walk gate to her property.

"Now what?" she asked. Darlene glanced at her watch. It was ten in the morning. Long after everyone that wanted water was supposed to be getting it. She went around the house and stepped through the side gate. Darlene saw the Doctor, Bear, and three other men.

Darlene walked over, but made no move to open the gate. "What is it?" she asked.

"We have another problem," the Doctor said. "Garbage is starting to pile up and…"

"For crying out loud! Just get a couple of guys to start up a garbage truck, load it up, compress the load and dump it at the dump. What's hard about that?"

Bear looked a bit sheepish. "Well, when you put it like that, nothing. We were talking about digging a hole and burying it here, using pickup trucks to gather it up."

"That's not at all efficient," Darlene said.

"No, it isn't; that's why we came to you," said one of the other men. One she didn't know. "Everybody says you always have an idea."

"Yeah, I have ideas, all right. But you don't want to hear some of them right at this moment."

"Come on, guys," Bear said. "I think I can figure out a garbage truck if we can find one." The group started to move away.

Darlene thought Dr. James was going to stay and say something else to her, but he shook his head and went with the others.

Later that day Darlene got on her bicycle and rode around the tract. Sure enough, there was Bear, driving the garbage truck, with the Doctor and one other man pitching the bags of trash and garbage up into the hopper. Every few stops Bear dumped the hopper into the tank and ran the ram to compress the load.

Darlene stopped. "Dr. James, you shouldn't be doing this! You're way too valuable to the community to catch something from handling this stuff, to straining your back, or something equally debilitating." She looked at the other man. "No offense."

The man smiled and replied. "None taken. I happen to agree with you. But no one else would volunteer to do it."

Darlene suddenly took a closer look at the man. "Are you… Are you Jim Haynes? The well driller?"

The man smiled and nodded. "Well, I don't really consider myself a real well driller. I jet in shallow wells for garden irrigation and for farmers to fill their water tanks out in the fields."

"You were the one I talked to and suggested I use a drive point to get water."

"Yeah! I remember that now! What did you ever do?"

"Drove two of them, as a matter of fact. The one everyone is using and…" Her eyes suddenly cut to the Doctor. He was smiling slightly at her inadvertent slip about having a second well.

She looked back at Jim. "Yeah. It worked fine." Suddenly excited, Darlene asked, "You still have the equipment to do it? Jet in wells?"

"Well, sure. But I don't have any materials. Things were so tough before this happened I quit stocking strainers, pipe, and fittings."

"But you could drill wells for the houses here, if we got you the materials?"

"Sure. Probably wouldn't need but one well for four or five houses, if the water flow is good."

Bear had left the truck and was listening in.

"Both of mine pump really easy and there is a full spout of water with every stroke." Darlene's face fell. "But we'd have to get pumps… And they'd need electricity…"

"It's doable," Jim interjected. "I know there are still some pumps where I was buying them for resell. We'd just need to find some portable generators. People would have to limit their water use to a couple of periods a day, so the generators wouldn't have to run all the time. You'd be able to get water, have light, cool down the fridge and freezer…"

Jim was getting excited. But his face suddenly fell. "But… Gee… I feel like a heel… But I have to figure a way to get food and stuff. Things are getting hard to find. Some of the ones without families are going far and wide to gather things up, but they want to get paid for them.

I… I'd need to get paid for the work I do, to buy food, since I wouldn't be able to go out salvaging."

"That's understandable," Bear said. "I kind of feel the same way. I think the community should pitch in and help the ones that are working for the good of the community. Like us, doing the garbage."

"I don't mind doing it," Dr. James said. "And I certainly won't refuse to treat someone if they don't have any money. What can we really buy with it, anyway?"

"Nothing. At the moment," Darlene said. "It would pretty much just be trade goods for services, services for services, and services for goods, and goods for other goods. After that… Well… there is something… But it's too early to talk about it. I'm certainly willing to contribute to the community coffers, and to pay individuals for any work they do for me."

"What do you say, Jim?" asked Dr. James. "If we get food for you in trade, and we can get the materials, you'd do the wells?"

"Absolutely!"

"The sooner the better, then," Darlene said. "This getting water from my hand pump is already getting really old. Half of them expect me to pump it for them. Even had one ask me to carry the bucket back for them."

"I guess we need to get some kind of formal organization going to get this done," Bear said. "A community council of sorts. A council in charge of a town meeting."

"Anyone even tries to resurrect the old CC&R's and I'm out. I mean it! This place had so many restrictions you wouldn't believe it."

"But you'd participate?" Dr. James asked.

"Sure she will, won't you, Darlene?" Bear asked.

"Actually," said Jim, "I think she should be nominated for council chair, assuming we'll do a vote and all."

"Not on your life!" Darlene said. "I'm not about to get involved in a mess like that. I'll go along, as long as things are well thought out and reasonable. And don't impact me much. I'll contribute to the community coffer, like I said before, but I'm not going to carry this place just because of a few people not wanting to lift a finger of their own."

"You're talking about Jayne Noodles," Dr. James said.

"That's one of them, for sure."

"She likes to throw her weight around and has a negative opinion about just about everything," Jim said.

"Yeah." Bear agreed, too.

"If I keep her out of your hair, you'll consider participating?" asked Dr. James.

Darlene hesitated, but finally nodded. "You keep her out of my hair and I'll participate. But not as an elected official! Just as a citizen with her own opinions to contribute."

That seemed to settle the matter. Bear headed back to get in the cab of the garbage truck, and the Doctor and Jim went to the next house to pick up their trash. Darlene got back on her bike and took off. All three of the others thought a similar thought. Like Darlene was on a mission.

They weren't wrong. Darlene went home, got the Marlin and a bandoleer of ammunition to add to the Redhawk she always carried, and headed for the entrance of the development at a rapid pace on the Paratrooper bicycle. Her first stop was at a Chevy/GMC dealership. She looked the vehicles over and picked a one-ton, crew-cab, four-wheel-drive, diesel powered pickup truck. It was all decked out for heavy off road use, with a heavy bumper and winch, and auxiliary lights pointed in every direction.

It took a few minutes to find the keys, and then Darlene got in the truck and started it up. The engine rattled for a few moments but settled down immediately. Darlene checked the fuel gauge and frowned. Less than an eighth of a tank. But suddenly she grinned. The sticker on the window had listed as an option two fuel tanks, the main tank fairly large. One-eighth of it should get done what she wanted.

With the bicycle in the bed of the truck Darlene headed for the tool rental place just down the road. She was a bit bruised afterwards, but had a portable generator loaded into the back of the truck a little while later. The place sold tools, as well as rented them. After going through what was available, Darlene put together a large toolbox full of hand tools.

She had to unload part of it to get the box up into the bed of the truck, but she managed, reloaded the toolbox, and then tied it and the generator off with load straps so they couldn't slide around on the coated bed.

Another short distance and she pulled into a service station that sold on road diesel fuel. It took her a solid four hours to figure out the wiring for the pump stations and the generator and get them hooked together so she could pump fuel.

After getting the pumps working she filled up both fuel tanks of the truck, and then disconnected the generator, leaving the leads she'd brought out of the wiring box where they were so it wouldn't take long to hook back up.

Next stop was a welding supply shop. She'd read her share of PAW fiction and knew how to get past difficult obstacles to get to what was wanted. With a cutting torch set secured in the bed of the truck, and several extra bottles of acetylene and plenty of oxygen bottles, along with some other items, Darlene went salvaging.

First salvaging stop was the closest coin shop. All she needed to get into it was an eight-pound sledgehammer, and a few healthy swings. She didn't go out of her way to destroy anything, but she was determined to get into the display cases and the large free standing safe in the back room of the store.

The display cases were easy. A pry bar was all that was needed. Darlene was selective. Only pre-1965 US silver coins, and gold coins of all types. When she had those in the truck she tackled the safe. Several blows of the sledgehammer didn't open it, though it sure wrecked the lock mechanism.

After thanking her father silently for having taught her 'boy stuff', when she was in her teens, Darlene put on cutting goggles, rolled the wheeled cart with the cutting torch into the shop and cut the lock off the safe. A few blows of the sledge and the guts of the mechanism fell into the safe and she was able to jiggle the locking studs so she could open the door. She was glad she'd taken the time. That was where the good stuff was. Like many others, the coin shop owner had held onto the majority of his precious metals. They were in the safe.

She left the high value non-precious metal numismatic coins for later collection by a history team she fully intended to organize, and took the precious metal bullion coins, rounds, and bars.

A gun store was down the street and she hit it next. Darlene worked until midnight and then found a store with some food left and ate a midnight snack. After a long nap in the locked up truck, she went to her next destination. She took another break the next morning, and then got right to it. By the time she pulled in to her house the next night just before midnight, the bed of the truck, and the U-Haul trailer she was pulling, were loaded down with guns, ammunition, gold, platinum, and silver.

The guns and ammo were the volume. The precious metals were the major value, though Darlene was pretty sure the guns and ammo would eventually have a great deal of value, too. By daybreak everything was stored away. She hadn't noticed the ladder on each side of her front fence during the night, but she saw it that morning as people began to approach for the morning water run. They must have found ladders somewhere that first evening or morning after so they could get to her well.

Darlene took her time looking over the house. Sure enough, there were signs of where someone had tried to get in. But they hadn't tried very hard, for the security shutters on every door and window showed only minor scratches.

She unlocked the front walk gate and let the people in. They were very quiet, staring at Darlene's dirty, disheveled appearance. Especially standing there with the Marlin slung over one shoulder and the ammunition bandoleer over the other, and the big revolver on her hip. She just stood there and watched as one person or family after another got water. The last ones to show up were Jayne and Kevin, Bear and his wife Julie, Jim, and Dr. James.

"You been rolling around in a pig sty?" Jayne asked coldly as Kevin pumped and Jim held the milk bottle for him. "Where have you been?" Jayne then asked when Darlene made no response to Jayne's first question.

"I'm a bit curious about that, myself," Dr. James said. "We thought something happened to you." His voice was more than a bit chiding.

"I'm a big girl, Doc. Don't need a keeper. I go where I want, when I want, how I want, and for the reasons I have."

Not until Jayne and Kevin were up the sidewalk quite a distance did she relax. "If you must know," she told Dr. James, "I simply went shopping."

"For what? Coal?" asked Jim with a laugh.

Darlene smiled. "That's on the next trip."

"I see you got a new ride in the process," Bear said, pumping for Jim, and then for his wife, and finally, for the Doctor.

"Did for a fact," Darlene said rather cheerfully. "Got a good deal on it, too. Now, since everyone has the water, I'm going to excuse myself, take down the ladders, and then go clean up and take a long nap. I don't expect to be disturbed by anyone or anything." She started to turn away, toward the house, but turned back.

Her demeanor was no longer light or her words bantering. "It would probably be best if I never find out who tried to get into my house. I might just take punitive action on whoever did it." With that, Darlene walked toward the house, triggering the security remote to open the front door security shutter, and then lock the gate behind the others when they went their separate ways with their water.

For the next seven days Darlene disappeared after the morning water haul, and got back just before the afternoon water haul. On that seventh day Dr. James told her that things were set up for a town meeting to elect a community council to lead it.

"Let me know how it goes," Darlene said and turned away.

"Come on, Darlene! Participate at least enough to show up." Darlene heard the humor in the Doctor's voice when he added, "You wouldn't want to get elected in absentia, would you?"

Darlene growled slightly and turned back. "I'll be there. Where and when?"

"Tomorrow at noon, in the community center."

"Okay. Like I said, I'll be there."

Other than a couple of the older teens and the children the teens were babysitting, everyone that had moved into the tract, plus a few that were living outside the tract, but nearby, showed up.

Darlene had to admit, Dr. James had a great speaking voice and manner. He held the group spellbound as he expounded on what was needed for the community to persevere and prosper. One of those things being the need for cooperative community action, strictly a democratic town hall meeting directed by a small council with a chairman and secretary.

Jim called out, "I nominate you, Doc, for chairperson."

"I second," Bear said.

"I move we elect Dr. James to the position of chairman of the council by acclimation," Darlene found herself saying, and began to clap her hands. Bear and Jim joined right in and in a few moments well over eighty percent were clapping.

Darlene stepped up and rapped the tabletop with her knuckles. "Dr. James is elected Chair of the Council by acclimation." She turned to him and said, "It's all yours now, Doc."

"We'll open the nominations for secretary of the Council now. Any nominations. Everyone was looking around at everyone else.

Suddenly Darlene heard Kevin's voice. "I nominate my wife, Jayne."

There was a second offered after a short pause, and then silence. "For lack of other nominations, I move we elect Jayne by acclimation," Dr. James said, keeping his eyes well away from Darlene.

A beaming Jayne made her way up to the table beside Dr. James. She sat down and slid the notepad and pencil that was on the table near her. She flipped open the notepad and began to write.

"Better vote on how many council members before we start nominating, hadn't we?" Bear asked.

Several people shouted out numbers, but the majority number was five.

"Can I see a show of hands for five members on the council?"

Darlene looked around at the group and had to agree with Dr. James when he said, "Motion carried. There will be five additional members of the board. That gives us an uneven number so there shouldn't be any deadlocks. Now, the floor is open to nominations for the five council member positions."

Bear and Jim both called out Darlene's name. After glaring at both of them when they seconded each other's nomination, she stepped up, raised her voice, and said, "I respectfully decline the nomination, and nominate Bear… that is, Randy Johanovich and Jim Haynes."

"One nomination to a person," Jayne said.

"Oh, I think we can be pretty lax on some of Robert's Rules. Other nominations, please."

There were only five nominations in total, so all were elected by acclamation.

Dr. James tapped the table. "Okay people! The elections are over. I think we council members should talk to all of you and get some idea of what we need and want to do. We can have a town hall meeting this Friday afternoon. Does someone so motion?"

"I so motion," someone called out.

People began to separate into small groups. Darlene suddenly noticed that Jayne was talking animatedly to two of the women that had been elected to the council. They were out of earshot, but Darlene could tell that Jayne was giving them an earful. "Probably about me," she whispered, "From the looks the three are giving me."

Darlene turned around. Doc, Jim, and Bear were talking together. The seventh man on the council was talking to a small group of people that had gathered around him.

"Oh," Darlene said, stepping up close to Dr. James, "You have so much trouble on your hands. I should have nominated you for King. Would have been easier. You have my best wishes."

Darlene left the three men and went home on her bicycle to get a little additional rest. The salvage work she'd been doing was tiring, and there were still the small stock, orchard, and greenhouse to take care of.

Again she made herself scarce for the next few days, continuing her salvage work alone. She'd added loose diamonds to her list of things to look for, but only a very narrow category. 1.0 to 1.1 carat, round brilliant cut, VVS 1 or better clarity, E or better color, with an attached GIA certificate. She didn't find all that many, but there were some in a few of the upscale jewelry stores. She also picked up a few other things in the stores, but the diamonds were the targeted items.

Come Friday morning, Dr. James, Bear, and Jim hung around the gate as everyone else got their morning water supply. Darlene acknowledged their presence with a nod, but none of the three made any effort to engage her in conversation.

At least, not until they had their water containers filled and set back outside the fence. Darlene was in the process of locking the gate when Dr. James said, "Can you hold on a minute, Darlene? We need to talk to you."

With a deep sigh Darlene leaned against the fence and asked, "Okay. What now?"

"We've… The council members," Bear said, "have talked to everyone else about what the council should be doing. Except you. We need your opinions for the town hall meeting this afternoon."

"You pretty well know what I believe," Darlene replied.

"In a haphazard way," Dr. James said. "We'd kind of like a… oh… 'official' list from you. We value your opinions and expertise."

"Yeah. Right," Darlene scoffed. "Okay. Give me a few minutes and I'll go over my own notes and write out a list of the things I've been hoping to do. Will you be at the community center?" The question was directed at Dr. James.

He nodded.

"Give me an hour," Darlene said. With that, the men picked up their water buckets and split up. Darlene went back into the house and turned on her laptop. She'd been keeping notes, as she'd told Dr. James and the others, about various projects she wanted to do, or see done. She rewrote the list, leaving out the more random thoughts about the projects, adding only the gist of the project.

Considerably less than an hour after their conversation, Darlene rode her bicycle down to the community center with the printed list in the backpack she took with her everywhere. She found all three men, Ed Hastings the fourth man on the council, plus Jayne and the other two women on the council going over each other's notes.

Ignoring Jayne, which was returned in kind, Darlene handed her three page list to Dr. James, turned, and started to leave.

"Don't you want to go over these and explain?" the Doctor asked.

"I think they're self-explanatory. At least enough so to figure out if you want to pursue them or not."

"Will you be at the meeting?" Bear asked.

Jayne did speak up then. "It's not required."

Darlene had already decided she wasn't going to go, but Jayne's words changed her mind. "Of course I will." With that she left before anyone could say anything else to her. As she went out the front door of the community center she was sure there was an argument going on among the council members.

She spent the rest of the day working at her place, harvesting from the gardens and orchards, and canning much of the produce. She was running out of places to store things. Her third bedroom was almost floor to ceiling with stored items.

Well before time for the town hall meeting, Darlene finished up what she was doing, took a shower, and dressed in fresh clothes. With a small smile on her face, she wrapped the gun belt around her waist and settled the Redhawk in the holster again. Small pack on her back, Darlene got the bicycle out of the garage and headed into what she was sure would be a fray.

It was. The meeting, with almost three quarters of the tract's residents in the audience, started off fairly well. Many people had come up with good ideas. Along with some ridiculous ones. All were discussed and either noted for future action, or dismissed out of hand.

Many of those dismissed seemed to have personal meaning for Jayne. She was frowning and getting visibly upset as item after item she voted for, was voted down, usually by a four to three margin, with Dr. James having to break deadlock after deadlock.

Darlene was beginning to get a little annoyed that not a single one of her suggestions had been addressed. But that changed in the blink of an eye. She recognized the printed list she'd given Dr. James.

Jayne immediately called for the meeting to adjourn so the council could consider the things they'd already gone over. It was voted down immediately.

She then called to handle the remaining agenda items in closed session. Again her suggestion was voted down.

"Okay," Dr. James said, "We have a package of suggestions from Darlene Carpenter." The room fell silent, as opposed to the constant murmurs that had been coming from the audience regularly.

Dr. James read the list. After he stopped, in the slight pause before anyone else could speak, Bear said, "I move we adopt all of these suggestions as goals for the community and pursue them as quickly as we can."

"Objection!" Jayne said. "We handled each of the other suggestions individually. I move we consider these in the same way. Put it to an open community vote."

"All those that believe these suggestions be considered as a package, raise your hand." Then, "All those that believe these suggestions be considered one-by-one, raise your hand."

It was close. One-by-one won out by three votes. Dr. James read off the first of Darlene's suggestions. It was to install septic tanks for the houses. Put on the to-do list.

Put in water wells, pumps, and generators. Put on the to-do list.

Require everyone to have a garden. Some major discussion on it. Put on the to-do list, with exceptions.

Set up an organized salvaging operation. Put on the to-do list.

Set up a community coffer and come up with reasonable assessments and payments for doing the community projects. Private projects would be on a one-to-one basis. A great deal of discussion. Tabled for future consideration.

There were additional items on the list, but the hour was getting late and everyone was ready to go get water and then go home. The remaining items on Darlene's list were tabled for future consideration.

Darlene hurried home to get ready for the onslaught of those getting water from her well. Things had gone rather better than she thought they would. Jayne's constant negativism, especially if the subject had any connection to Darlene, was not well received by the majority.

"But," Darlene warned herself, "She does have a small power base and intends to make my life miserable."

As they had that morning, Dr. James, Bear, and Jim hung around until the others had their water and had left.

"That went fairly well," Dr. James said, smiling.

"Not as well as it could have," Bear said. "But not bad."

Jim didn't comment on the meeting directly. He did say, "Darlene, I hate to ask, but I'm going to need help getting the things for the wells."

"That should be handled, by rights," Darlene said, "by the community salvage teams." She paused. "But, if it goes the way I think it will, I'll help you the best I can."

"Thanks, Darlene. Now I have to figure out how much to charge."

"Can't help you there, Jim. You'll have to make your own deals with each person or head of household."

Jim sighed. "That Noodles woman told me her well would be my first one. And since she's on the council, the council would pay out of the public coffers."

"Why am I not surprised?" Darlene said.

Dr. James' face fell. "I didn't know that. That's not going to happen. Each household that wants a well will have to pay for it on their own. If we let even one person do something like that the council will be paying for everything."

"And," Bear interjected, "You know good and well that setting and collecting assessments is going to be a real pain."

"And you wondered why I didn't want to participate!" Darlene said with a small laugh. Then, seriously, she added, "But, unless Jayne gets a say and demands my entire property, you won't have a problem collecting from me. Give me a reasonable assessment and I'll fork it right over, to get things started. Maybe it'll influence a few. Though I'd just as soon how much of what I contribute not be public knowledge. Only that I did contribute."

"That might be difficult, but we'll try," Dr. James said. "To be honest, I really don't know how to make such an assessment. I'm not comfortable with Jayne's suggestion of those with the most give, and those that have very little be exempted."

"You start that, you have the same situation you mentioned, Doc. No one will admit to having anything, and will want to receive everything they can from those that obviously have. Like me."

"Just how much do you have?" Dr. James asked. He realized his casual comment wasn't taken casually by Darlene immediately. She darted him a disappointed look, spun on her heel, and marched, back straight and stiff, to her front door. She went in and the security shutter started downward.

"Man, you stepped in it that time, Doc," Bear said.

"I hope to tell yah," added Jim.

"I'm afraid you're right," admitted Dr. James. "I wasn't really asking. Not really. Just curious. Like the rest."

"You don't want to be considered, 'like the rest' in her eyes. She doesn't think too much of most of them. She was prepared for this to a great degree and none of the rest of us were. Why should she even try to help? We didn't help ourselves when we could, the way she did." It was a long speech for Bear.

"You really need to straighten this out, Doc," Jim said.

With a sad nod, Dr. James agreed. The three split up and headed back to their homes.

The next day, during the morning drinking water run, Darlene took Jim aside. "As soon as you can, come back here and we'll start looking for what you need to start jetting in some wells."

"Okay, Darlene. And thanks. I know you don't really have to do this."

"I want to. You've been one of the few really doing everything you can to make things better for everyone."

"Well… I don't know about how helpful I've been. But I do try. Okay. I'll be back in half an hour or so."

Like Jim, Darlene had gone through the yellow pages looking for possible suppliers of the necessary components to get people water supplies.

It took all day, and they had to stop at several establishments all over the city, and some quite a ways out of it, but they found what they needed for Jim to get started. Which he did that very next day.

One of his friends forked over some canned goods and Jim jetted in the thirty foot well, hooked up a pump, plumbed it to the house piping, and hooked the pump to a generator. Long extension cords were run inside to power up a few electrical items for the times the generator was running to operate the water pump.

That transaction broke the ice and others began to make offers of various goods or services to get their own water and power system installed. There were several cases where one well and generator worked for two adjacent homes, which greatly stretched the number of houses that could get the water and power.

Jim made it a point to give Darlene some of what he collected, despite her protestations, for the help she had provided. Finally, Darlene accepted, realizing it was another precedent that needed to be set.

Jim didn't turn Jayne into a friend when he continued to refuse to put her system in, and bill the council. Eventually Kevin went to him and made the arrangements, forking over the now standard amount of canned and packaged food.

After two weeks of work Jim had everyone water in their home, and at least a little bit of electrical power on an intermittent basis. Jayne was one of the ones that tried to run the generator constantly and ruined the generator that Jim had provided. When she demanded Jim replace it with a new one, Jim declined. Jayne and Kevin were on their own to get a replacement.

The water systems were a double edged sword. With running water people again tried to use the flush toilets, with the same result they'd had before. The city sewers simply weren't going to work in the foreseeable future.

Jim, with a couple of the other men that had started helping him, including Bear, started correcting the situation by installing individual septic systems for each house. Again Darlene, now a very skilled locator and salvager, helped round up the materials needed.

Bear loaded the prefab septic tanks onto a delivery truck, and then unloaded them into the hole he'd dug for that system. The sewer line from the house to the city sewer was cut and plumbed into the tank, and a leech field was installed using leech pipe and plenty of gravel.

The first installation was at Darlene's. The systems went in as fast as Darlene could find new sources of the materials. Again Jayne was a problem. She didn't want the front yard disturbed. "Put it in the back yard," she insisted.

Kevin finally managed to get it through her head that the new septic system had to go where the existing sewer pipe could connect to it. Due to the hassles, their system was one of the last to go in. Again with a request to bill the council. Kevin paid up after a day's salvaging on his own.

The other problem the water systems caused was a drastically higher need for gasoline to fuel the generators. Every system had included two five-gallon jerry cans of gasoline to get the systems going. Many people ran through what they had without consideration of where they'd get more.

Darlene's spirit of free enterprise stepped in again to fill the need. While she'd been fueling up regularly at the same station she'd used the first time, she'd made no provisions to supply the tract.

She hired two men desperate to feed their families to run the station for her, dispensing gasoline and diesel from the pumps, which were all now connected to a larger generator. The generator was on wheels and could be moved to another station when the first one ran dry.

Darlene kept ten-percent of what was taken in and let the two guys split the rest. Again, most of the payment was in salvaged food and other products. Just about every family was now regularly salvaging on their own. Dr. James' attempts to set up organized salvaging for the community, as Darlene had suggested, came to naught.

One day not long after she'd made fuel easily available, she was taking a tour of the tract to see how the septic systems were going, and suddenly noticed that just about every driveway had some type of new vehicle in it. Often two or three. Only the biggest, best, most expensive cars, trucks, and SUV's.

"Can't say much, I guess," Darlene told herself. "I did the same." It just seemed a waste to her. She only used the Chevy one-ton to haul things that wouldn't fit in the Subaru. And she used the Paratrooper bicycle for most trips in the tract or close by when she didn't need to carry something that wouldn't fit in her pack.

Darlene also discovered that the easy pickings for salvaging were long gone. All the stores and other local establishments had been picked over. Mostly haphazardly. Darlene started her own campaign of organized salvage of the picked over places. With a couple of people helping her for a percentage, she began gathering up everything left that could have any conceivable use later on.

The two people helping her only helped her load. They were dropped off when she was ready to unload the truck and the trailer she used for salvage. Darlene didn't want anyone to know where she was storing the stuff. It wasn't at her house. There just wasn't room.

There was a self-storage facility some distance away. She was able to get the gate open without too much trouble and chose half a dozen of the larger empty units to begin storing her salvage in. Darlene put her own chain and lock on the gate of the storage facility to keep any casual visitors out.

Only things that extreme heat or cold could hurt did she take home to store. The second bedroom of the three in the house was beginning to fill. Everything else, with few exceptions, went into one of the storage rooms.

The temperatures the last few days had been in the mid-sixties. Quite comfortable. And the skies seemed to have a bit less contamination in them now, though they were in no way clear. The garden, even the greenhouse, had suffered some due to the lack of light.

At the next town hall meeting, which she reluctantly attended, again in self-defense, Darlene noticed the many flashes of light out in the audience. She looked a little closer. Seemed like every woman there was loaded down with jewelry. And the way it was reflecting the light coming through the windows, it was the real thing. "SUV's aren't the only thing being salvaged, I guess," Darlene told herself. Then she smiled slightly. "No different than me. I'm just not wearing much of what I took."

Suddenly she felt a chill and looked back at the door. Several people were coming in. A breezed followed them in. Darlene realized it was much cooler than any since before the impacts. "This is not good," she said softly.

Things seemed to be going well for the community and the town hall meeting went quickly. Just before Dr. James was ready to adjourn the meeting, Darlene raised her hand.

"Chair recognizes Darlene Carpenter."

"I hate to bring this up, but I think we're in for a severe winter. Probably well past time to start thinking of getting heat for everyone."

"You have got to be kidding!" someone in the group called out. "It's been hotter than you know what for months!"

"I feel an attempt to gouge the council and her fellow citizens with another crazy scheme," Jayne said loudly."

Darlene frowned and said, "Never mind. No one wants to think about it, no skin off my nose."

She was almost out the door when she heard the gavel that had been located for Dr. James to use, and a hurried. "Meeting adjourned."

Dr. James, Bear, and Jim caught up with her before she got inside her house.

"Darlene! Wait! We want to talk to you."

Darlene almost went inside. She knew she was being overly sensitive. If it had only been Jayne's remark, Darlene probably would have pressed the matter. But with the other comments, accepted by so many of the others, the head in the sand attitude had really gotten under her skin.

"Okay," she said as she turned around and walked back down to the front fence. "What?"

"What you were saying…" Dr. James said. "Well… It's so hard to believe that…"

Darlene started to head back for the house. "Let me rephrase that," Dr. James said. Darlene faced the three men again.

"Could you explain further what you were talking about earlier?"

"There are theories that after a strike, or series of strikes like we took, there would be a period of very high temps."

"We sure had that," Bear said.

"Yes we did. And there are theories that the high temperatures would last for many years. They haven't. Which brings me to another theory. The one that says as the temperatures slowly drop due to minimal sunlight reaching the earth. That, though the cloud cover can hold the temperatures up for a while because of slower than usual loss of heat to space, the lack of sunlight will over ride that and temperatures will drop."

"They have done that," Jim chimed in.

"A lot. A whole lot. Several degrees below normal. Around the entire earth."

"You're not saying a mini-ice age, much less a full scale ice-age, are you?" asked Dr. James.

"That's exactly what I'm saying. At the very least, very severe winters, probably starting with this one, and a year without summer. I'm not as confident of a mini-ice age or full ice-age."

"We don't need anything else to worry about," Dr. James said, looking down at the ground.

"Then don't," Darlene replied. "I was just trying to give the council the benefit of my opinions, just as I was asked."

"We did ask," Jim said to Dr. James.

"Of course we did," Dr. James replied, looking at Darlene. "And we welcome them. But just like the high heat… What can we possibly do if there is even just a really severe winter. There's no natural gas, and the small generators we have won't run electric heaters. Even if we could find enough fuel."

"There has to be a way," Jim said.

"Wood, of course," Bear said. "We can install wood stoves in the houses and cut wood. We have an entire national forest we can cut down for firewood."

"Well, I wouldn't want to take it that far," Darlene replied. "And unless I miss my guess, we would be hard pressed to get enough wood cut for everyone for the winter, even if we could find and install, safely, mind you, wood heating and cooking stoves in every house.

"But there is an alternative. Every house, I think, in this entire suburb is on natural gas."

"Of which there is none," Dr. James said.

"Give me a chance, will you?" Darlene asked sharply. "Most appliances that use natural gas can be converted to propane. Most of the rural area uses propane. It shouldn't be that hard to acquire propane tanks for everyone, and convert heaters, hot water heaters, and cook stoves to propane. There should be enough electrical power to run the blowers on the heaters. Again, it would have to be just for a few hours in the morning, and a couple in the evening. Low thermostat settings, and everyone wears a sweater inside the house."

"I had thought about getting small propane heaters that mount on the small tanks, but what you're talking about would be much better," Jim said.

"Count me in," Bear said, "No matter what anyone else does. But we need to think about wood heat for everybody in the future. The propane won't hold out forever."

"My thought exactly," Darlene said. "I have instructions on how to convert in my laptop. I'll print them out. Between them, and what we can learn at a propane dealership, we should be able to train at least two or three people to do the conversions."

The others were nodding. Darlene started speaking again. "You guys decide who is going to do what. I'll take it on myself to provide the propane. Free of charge for the first fill of each tank. After that, it'll cost if I provide the fuel. That isn't saying anyone else can't get propane on their own. Competition is a good thing, in my opinion."

The others nodded again, not surprised at Darlene's introduction of financial aspects into the discussion.

During the last week of October, when everything had been gathered up to convert the appliances, people began to wonder if Darlene might be right. The temperature had continued to fall, every day. It was now in the forties and keeping warm at night meant lots of blankets.

Darlene, with two others helping her again, had a semi-trailer load of five-hundred-gallon propane tanks at the tract, along with two ten-wheel delivery trucks. With Bear helping with a mobile crane, the tanks were unloaded and set at each house, and then filled, in three days.

A three-thousand-gallon commercial tank Darlene found was placed in her yard, and a fifteen-hundred-gallon tank placed at the community building.

The process of converting the appliances began, but it went slowly. Again, Darlene's were done first as an example.

Unlike the conversion from propane to natural gas, where existing orifices could be drilled out for use, new orifices had to be found and installed. There just simply weren't enough of them to go around. New, propane fired, appliances were taken off showroom floors and out of warehouses and installed in several of the homes, after the natural gas appliances were removed.

While the work was on going, Darlene moved a pair of propane fired whole house generators from the propane place and installed them in her back yard. Bear moved them with the portable crane, as he had the propane tank. He was now the only one that knew for sure what Darlene had in her back yard.

She plumbed the generators in and wired them up, leaving the original system in place for back up, with the hundred pound bottles connected. Darlene had made sure that her commercial tank had a wet leg so she could fill the smaller bottles and tanks. Darlene's house was now in basically the same shape, in terms of utilities, as before the meteor strikes.

The third large generator that the propane supply had she took to the community center and installed it so they would have electrical power, as well as heat, running water, and sewer. Darlene did a salvage run to gather up maintenance items for the three generators, to keep them running for years of moderate use. They should last as long as the propane held out, if they weren't abused.

During a town meeting to fill everyone in on the progress being made, Darlene brought up some new business. "I'd like to buy the vacant lot next to me," she said when she'd been recognized by Dr. James.

Several called out, "Just use it! Nobody else is!"

It was one time that Jayne and Darlene agreed on something. Jayne immediately said, "She must pay for it. It's community property by default."

"But she's already given the community all the stuff to get the community center back up to speed. That should be enough," said someone else.

"I want to pay for it, separately," Darlene said. "I want free and clear title so there won't be any questions about it later."

"What do you want it for?" Jayne asked.

"Personal business," replied Darlene coldly.

"It doesn't matter," Dr. James said. "All those in favor of selling the property to Darlene, raise your hand."

There were only a few dissenting votes. "Now, about how much?" Jayne asked. "That is very valuable property we're talking about. And with cash not worth much of anything, we're going to need to come to some equitable form of payment."

"I'm willing to add to the community coffers the amount of food an average person would eat in a year under current circumstances."

"You have that much?" Jayne asked. She looked livid.

"Have or can get," Darlene said easily.

"That sure would let us pay for things the community wants done, but no one will volunteer to do," said Jim. "Let's vote on it. Doc."

"All those in favor of accepting the offered payment raise your hand, please." It was another case of only two or three negative votes.

"Has the council decided on any recommendations for the amount of contribution each resident is going to give to the community? I'd like to get it out of the way so I know what I have available going into the winter."

There was a lot of discussion among the group.

"Order. Order." Dr. James said, tapping the gavel a couple of times on its sound block to get silence and attention back to the council table.

Jayne spoke up as soon as she could be heard. "I move that those that have prospered by the events of the past many weeks should contribute their fair share, which should be distributed to those of us that have worked tirelessly to make this community a better place to live, at the detriment of our own situations." She was glaring at Darlene.

Again pandemonium broke out and Dr. James banged his gavel, much louder this time. "Quiet, please! Quiet! This is something that must be discussed!"

"No discussion," Jayne yelled. "I call for a vote!"

"Vote!" "Vote!" "Vote!" rang out from all over the room.

Dr. James looked over at Darlene and gave a small shrug. Darlene was standing there, arms crossed, watching the crowd. Suddenly she spoke up. "Listen, people! Listen! I have something to say before you have a vote."

"There is to be no discussion!" Jayne yelled out.

"It won't be," Darlene said firmly. Silence fell at her statement, and Darlene made her statement. It was short. "All of you thinking of voting for this remember that you might be on the other end of that food chain in the future. Those willing to accept such spoils of banditry don't care who it comes from, as long as it's not from them, but to them."

Darlene dropped her arms to her side and headed for the door.

"Aren't you staying to see how the vote turns out?" called someone from the audience group.

Darlene looked at the man, and then surveyed the entire group, and the council members at their table. "It doesn't matter to me," she said. "Either way it doesn't affect me. Everything will be fine, or I will be gone, with my goods, my lot a scorched and salted piece of ground."

"You can't do that!"

Darlene didn't respond. She continued out the door and went home. Angrier and more disappointed than at any time in her life that she could remember.

It was a half an hour before the walkway gate buzzer sounded. She looked through the peephole of the door. "The Three Musketeers again," she muttered upon seeing Dr. James, Bear, and Jim.

She went out to talk to them. Bear spoke before the others did. "It was close. But Noodles lost. The vote was not for the haves to give to the have-nots. Everyone is to give one month of food for one person to the community for community works."

The three men looked at Darlene expectantly. After a few moments she asked, "What? You expect me to comment? I meant what I said. It doesn't matter to me. Anyone that tries to take what I've built here without my permission will be dealt with harshly. If there is a significant attempt, I'll leave, just like I said I would."

"Please don't be hasty," Dr. James said. "Give us a chance to work on a situation before you make rash decisions."

"I'll do as I please, within the bounds of common sense. My common sense. Not the group's, if it has any at all. But I don't want to see bad things happen here. I'll do my part. The part I decide I should do. The community will have thirteen months of food for one person tomorrow. Figure out how you're going to store it and protect it."

With that she turned and went back inside. The three didn't try to stop her this time.

"That is one ticked off lady!" Bear said.

"I think, with good reason," added Jim.

Dr. James said only, "I'll see you guys in the morning." He turned and headed for his house. The other two followed suit, each man keeping his thoughts to himself.

The next morning Darlene spent the early hours loading the pickup with twenty-six boxes. Each held a decent amount of food for two weeks for one person. It was mostly things she'd salvaged early on. She wasn't ready for it to be known her resources for animal protein. No one, other than Bear, except possibly Dr. James, even knew she had the chickens. The Doctor might have heard them and figured out they were in her back yard. She doubted anyone else would think so, unless she gave it away in some way.

Stopping at the community center she found all the council members there, including Jayne and Dr. James. "I've got it," Darlene announced. "Where do you want it?"

Jayne, an angry frown pasted on her face didn't say anything, though Darlene was sure she wanted to. "Here, I guess," Dr. James said. "We can put it in the storeroom and keep it locked. Come on, Bear, Jim. Let's get it unloaded."

Darlene stayed out of the way and let the three men move the boxes. When Bear said, "Man, you should see that Jayne! Oohing and ahing over every box. How it should be more. About how she…" he could have kicked himself and shut up quickly, grabbing another box without looking at Darlene.

"Don't worry," Jim said. "Doc's got the only keys."

"Not a worry in my head. Once it's in the council's hands, it's yours to do with as you please. Of course, I would be very disappointed if it was just handed out to those that asked for it, the way Jayne wanted to do."

"That isn't going to happen," Dr. James said, hearing what she said as he came out for another box."

When the truck was unloaded Darlene asked the three men, "You guys know where Craig and Travis are this morning?"

"I think they're putting up a clothes line for the Hostens," Bear said. "You have some work? I would sure like to build up my stocks for winter, considering what you think about the winter coming. Finding food now out in the world is getting really hard. My last food salvaging trip wasn't very successful."

"As a matter of fact, I can use all the useful help I can get. Sure, Bear."

"I'm in, if that's okay," Jim said.

The two men looked at Dr. James. Darlene spoke before he said anything. "He needs to be careful of his hands. This is going to be some rough work."

"Now you tell me," Bear said with a laugh.

"I'm going to have to risk them. Like the others, I don't have enough to get me through the winter."

"Well… There is something you can do that shouldn't endanger your hands. Meet me at my place. I'm going to go see if Travis and Craig will be available."

When Dr. James, Bear, and Jim showed up Darlene told them, "Travis and Craig are tied up for another day, so it's just going to be us." She loaded a Coleman cooler into the back of the truck. There was already a five-gallon water cooler in the truck. So were Darlene's wood cutting tools.

"Uh-oh," Bear said with a grin. "I may have spoken at the wrong time."

Dr. James climbed into the front bucket seat of the truck and Bear and Jim took the crew cab seat.

They rode in silence until Darlene pulled into one of the propane suppliers on the far side of the city. Everyone climbed out and Darlene said. "Okay, Doc. I've got five delivery trucks already filled up for future use. I want you to drive them to my vacant lot and park them. We'll be back with a load of wood and drop you off again. That okay?"

"Uh… Maybe you better wait a minute and let me see if I can get the thing in gear. I'm never driven anything this big."

Darlene, Bear, and Jim watched with some amusement as Dr. James got the feel of the smallest of the three trucks. He finally turned toward the gate after a

few start and stop attempts. He sounded the horn and
took the truck out on the road.

"I guess he's got it," Darlene said. "Let's go. Don't
want to keep him waiting too long."

Bear grabbed the front passenger seat and Jim took
the rear seat. It wasn't very far to the first place Darlene
had wood already cut and ready to load.

"You've been at this before, haven't you?" Bear
asked on seeing the neatly stacked firewood covered with
a tarp.

"Yeah. Wasn't sure it would still be here. Let's load
up."

It didn't take long to fill the trailer and the bed of the
truck, using a bucket brigade approach and tossing the
pieces of wood from one to the other. Darlene caught up
with the slow moving propane truck just before he turned
into the tract.

Darlene pulled the pickup and trailer to another
section of the empty yard while Dr. James parked the
propane delivery truck next to the two already on the lot.
As she, Bear, and Jim began to unload the firewood, Dr.
James walked over to watch and ask, "Are you sure you
want seven trucks full of propane sitting next to your
house?"

"I'm not so sure," Bear said. He was in the house on the other side of the vacant lot from Darlene.

"They won't be there long. I plan on moving them to a secure location. Parking them here is just temporary."

"Why didn't you just have me park them where you want them long term?" Dr. James asked.

Darlene just gave him a look.

"Oh," he said. Bear and Jim laughed.

"Okay. Time to go get another load each," Darlene said a few minutes later. "And Doc, we won't be back as quickly this time. Just hang loose until we get back, okay?"

Dr. James nodded and climbed into the pickup.

They moved three of the five propane trucks that day, and hauled three pickup and trailer loads of firewood, of which the last load had to be cut. It was all standing dead wood and would make good firewood without needing much drying time.

Over the next week, the other two propane delivery trucks were moved, first to the tract, and then Darlene moved them to the storage yard. There didn't seem to have been any activity other than hers at the storage yard. She moved two of the three trucks already from the vacant lot, leaving just one on the lot for use that winter without having to go get one. Beside it was parked a ten-wheel plus tag axle liquid fuel tanker with a split load of gasoline and diesel for easy access that winter, too.

With Craig and Travis helping in addition to Bear and Jim, using five chainsaws, a tremendous amount of firewood was cut, moved, and covered, with several more cords still in the forest to dry, also covered. There wasn't another tarp to be found anywhere.

Temperatures were now below freezing and the first snow came on November 1st. It was a dirty, grimy, grayish color, but it was snow. The midday sky was as dark as late twilight and the wind was light.

Darlene sat down at her communications and computer desk and turned on her Yaesu Amateur radio transceiver and began checking in with the list of contacts she had built up over the months.

When she turned the radio off late that evening, just before she went to bed, the ominous feeling she'd felt days before was now worse. Just about everyone she talked to in the Northern Hemisphere either had been receiving snow for the last few days, or it was just starting. North to South, East to West, the entire US was getting snow or the threat of it. The further south, the snow started a bit later, and was a bit less, but it was snowing all the way down in the Gulf of Mexico.

A shiver went down her back despite the cozy warmth of her house. If this was a sign of things to come, the small community was in for some bad times.

CHAPTER FIVE

-

The snow kept coming, off and on, for three months. Over eight feet of accumulation, with drifts in places twenty feet high, kept everyone except Darlene snowed in. Well, Darlene and whomsoever she offered one of the four snowmobiles she'd salvaged well before the winter set in.

Bear and Jim, at Darlene's suggestion, and the council's approval during another town meeting to address the issue, moved more of the construction equipment to the tract that could be used for snow removal. Just plowing it would have put hard packed snow ten feet deep in peoples' front yards, so the snow was loaded in a dump truck and dumped on the lots of those houses that still remained vacant and didn't have a front fence.

They could only do enough to make movement around the tract doable. The road past the gate house was one of the places with a twenty-foot drift. There weren't very many places anyone wanted to go, so no attempt was made to clear it, to conserve fuel.

The snows finally slowed in early February, though they continued, mostly as flurries. The skies had cleared except for the very highest and finest of debris, allowing a watery looking sunshine to reach the ground. Most of the tremendous amounts of moisture that the atmosphere had picked up due to the impacts, plus the evaporation because of the resultant heat, had finally been dropped as snow around the northern hemisphere as the temperatures fell and the air could no longer hold that moisture.

The lowest temperature Darlene saw on her weather instruments was ten below zero. But temperatures held around the zero mark for weeks after the snow had slowed to those occasional flurries. But with her greenhouse heated, and the increased sunshine, Darlene was able to double her production of greenhouse vegetables. Whereby came a problem.

Again it was centered on Jayne, along with a couple of her friends. Jayne believed that the fruits of Darlene's labors should be the property of the group, by some reasoning only she understood, but couldn't articulate.

There were half a dozen families nearly out of food, some having been on short rations for a month. The food that Darlene had contributed to the community coffers was almost all gone. A bit of it had gone to pay Bear, Jim, Craig, and Travis, the four men in the tract that had both the ability and willingness to do much of the hard work required by the community.

To complicate things, the Noodles had once again burned out their generator, leaving them without power, water, and heat. Rather than move in with one of the friends they had in the tract, Jayne had demanded, and received, permission to stay in the community building, since it had all the requisites for comfortable life in the winter. And, of course, until it ran out, a stash of food.

With production up, Darlene had started selling off some of her home canned goods, mostly for promises of labor when she wanted it, and the return of the empty jars. Jayne had refused, on Kevin's behalf, to enter into any such arrangement. Again she demanded free access to the rest of the supplies in the community center, and Darlene's supplies, stating that need outweighed any form of private ownership.

Nearly the entire population was in attendance of the town hall meeting that called to resolve the issue.

"We have to have food!" Jayne said as soon as Dr. James opened the meeting. "She…" Jayne continued, pointing at Darlene "has it. She should be banned from the tract and her supplies distributed to those of us that need them the most."

Pandemonium erupted, with people shouting their agreement or disagreement with Jayne's statement. After a few minutes of angry exchanges, which Darlene stayed completely out of, silence finally fell, and all eyes turned to Darlene when she spoke.

"Okay, people, let me lay this out in simple terms. What is mine is mine, to be done with as I see fit. I will defend it and myself if any attempt is made to take anything from me by force. Now, despite what has gone on, I am willing to provide a minimum amount of food, subsistence rations, for anyone that needs it. Through the council. I expect, in return, for the community to provide a labor pool, again, arranged through the council, to pursue my private ventures, once the opportunity comes for everyone to get out and fend for themselves again.

"I simply will not just give away what I worked and sweated for to accumulate over the years because some of you can't control yourselves, and aren't willing to work for your own subsistence. Anyone that wants to make a private deal, I will continue to do that. If you want a handout, see the council."

There was continued silence when Darlene quit speaking. For a few moments, anyway. Then pandemonium erupted again. Darlene thought Dr. James was going to break his gavel, pounding it the way he was to get quiet.

He finally had his quiet. But before he could speak, Jayne did. "Preposterous! Someone should grab her before she can pull that gun and…"

"That's enough!" Dr. James said, in a tone and volume not heard before from him. "It's simple. We vote on Mrs. Carpenter's offer. If it passes, it will be carried out. If not, further discussion will take place. Reasonable discussion. Without threats from any participant against any other. Now. Those in favor of Mrs. Carpenter's offer please raise your hand."

It wasn't particularly close, the offer was accepted, but a disappointing large number of people didn't raise their hand.

"I'll have some food here first thing in the morning. Don't expect surf and turf." With that, Darlene left the community center as people began discussing the events of the past few minutes, and Dr. James tried to get quiet again so he could adjourn the meeting.

Darlene was a bit surprised that Bear, Jim, and Dr. James didn't try to talk to her after the meeting. But since they didn't, Darlene went ahead and got to work to prepare for the next day. She knew exactly what she had stored, and where.

She moved several cases of home canned meat and vegetables to the living room, to make it easy to load into the truck the following morning. Then she went into the garage and carefully removed a panel in the wall connecting the shelter to the back wall of the garage. She worked her way slowly past the stacks of buckets and boxes crammed in the space head high.

It took her until midnight to get out what she wanted from the hidden compartment and put the panel back in place. She took a shower and went to bed, but tossed and turned the rest of the night. Restless and still tired when her alarm went off, Darlene dragged herself out of the comfortable bed and went about her morning routine. She was in no hurry to get to the community center. "Let them wait and worry," she mumbled as she sipped tea and listened to the chatter on the Amateur radio. Her community wasn't the only one suffering from problems, most of them related to the snow.

But she couldn't wait for long. She was too anxious to see how things would go. Bear and Dr. James seemed to be waiting for her to come out of her house, for both showed up at her gate minutes after she carried out the first box of canning jars full of rabbit.

"We came to help load," Dr. James said.

Just to get a bit of a dig in, Darlene said, "Not really that much to load. We're not talking five course meals here. I said subsistence rations and I meant it. But, since you're here, come on."

Darlene opened the driveway gate and the two men joined her. "I'll bring it out and you two can load it," she said when they got to her entry porch.

"Not going to let us in, huh?" Bear said. He was grinning.

Darlene wasn't. "Nope."

As she handed the boxes and buckets out, Dr. James and Bear loaded them into her pickup truck. One of the common snow flurries was sprinkling the containers with a fine layer of, finally, white snow, but it was blown away as quickly as it landed. The temperature was in the single digits and the wind was picking up.

When Darlene handed the last container out, she reached inside the door, picked up her Marlin and a bandoleer and carried them out to the truck after locking the door and dropping the security shutter.

"Is that really necessary?" Dr. James asked, nodding at the rifle and ammunition she put in the front seat of the Chevy one-ton.

"Let's hope not. Understand, Doc, that I am serious about protecting my goods and myself. You heard what Jayne said last night. To seize me and disarm me. Well, I'll tell you now, I will go down fighting. And if there is any way, if I think I'm doomed, I'll burn the house down with everything in it. Just for spite. That's just the way I am."

All the Doctor could do was nod in acknowledgement of her words. Bear and the Doctor climbed into the back of the truck with the supplies and Darlene headed for the community center.

There was a group waiting. Almost a mob, really, but not quite. There were plenty of hands to unload the truck and take it into the community center meeting room. Darlene, the rifle over one shoulder and the bandoleer over the other stood by the table that the food was stacked on and under.

When a couple of people came up and started to open the boxes, Darlene, fire in her eye, said, "I don't think so. The council will distribute this. Back off." She ignored the name the woman called her and stood her ground.

When Dr. James came in he asked for quiet. "Come on, people! The food just got here. Give the council a few minutes to see what we have here and get things organized."

Slowly the room emptied, except for the members of the council. Darlene wondered if anyone besides herself noticed Jim when he came in last. He had a handgun holstered on his hip, the same way Darlene did. Their eyes met and Jim winked at her. She smiled just slightly and gave a tiny nod.

Darlene turned to Bear and asked, "Would you help me set up the grinder?"

"Grinder?" Jayne asked. She'd been quiet up to that point, her eyes seldom leaving the boxes on the table.

"I have wheat," Darlene replied. "It's useable the way it is, but isn't that palpable to most. I'll grind it into flour so it can be baked into bread."

"I don't bake," Jayne said.

"Okay," was the only return comment.

Bear hoisted the heavy grinder onto the table and Darlene reached down and tightened the C-clamps to hold it in place. She pointed to one of the buckets. Can you open that one?" Darlene opened a box and handed him a bucket lid lifter.

Dr. James and the other council members were opening boxes and, with the lid lifter now, the buckets, taking a quick inventory.

"This is all?" Jayne asked finally. "And what kind of meat is that? If it's meat?"

"Rabbit," replied Darlene, "and fish."

"And what is this? Rice? Beans? And that one?"

"Yes. Rice, beans, and lentils. In various combinations they'll keep you going and stretch the meat and vegetables."

"But you've been selling chicken and eggs and fresh vegetables and canned fruit. Where is it?"

"Paying customers only."

"This is not acceptable!" Jayne said, her voice beginning to rise. "Dr. James! I demand she give us the best she has!"

Even her two friends on the council couldn't quite accept the demand. "Come on, Jayne," one of them said. "It's food. It'll get us through the winter. And then, I mean to tell you, I plan to have Harry out there every day looking for enough food to get us through the next winter. Regular food."

When Jayne didn't respond, Darlene told Dr. James, "You need to let people know they need containers to carry their portions. I don't have enough to go around, and I probably wouldn't get them back."

"Bear?" the Doctor said, "Would you go out and tell them?"

"Sure, Doc." Bear hurried toward the double doors of the entry into the meeting room and disappeared for several minutes.

Darlene, as she started using the Diamante 525 grinder to convert the wheat kernels to flour, noticed Dr. James and the others setting out groups of jars. "I hope that isn't what you plan to hand out for each person. What I brought today has to last everyone that gets it for a full week."

"This for a week? For everyone?" Jayne was screeching. "I thought it was for today! This is unacceptable, I tell you! Unacceptable!"

"Well, it's what you've got. And to tell you the truth, depending on how long this winter lasts, even I might not have enough for everyone."

Dr. James looked at her sharply, and Jayne and the other two women had mouth hanging open stares on their faces.

"But… But… You have so much!" Jayne protested.

"But not unlimited supplies, I assure you. Now, I would suggest one-pint jar of meat and one of fish for each person for the week. Three jars of vegetables, with rice and either beans or lentils filling out the menu. A cup of honey each. Some sugar, salt, and oil to make the other things useable.

"I almost didn't bring any, but I can't stand the thought of the children doing without, so, in addition to the honey there is some candy. The candy is for the children only. Three portions per, for the week."

For once, Jayne stayed silent as the others began to rearrange what they had set out for distribution. "One more thing," Darlene said, bringing an annoyed glance from her, "I want the jars and what containers I do provide, back. I don't get them back, and there won't be any more home canned goods."

"How do we know this food is safe? You say you canned it yourself. What about botulism?" It was Jayne again.

"I'm a safe canner!" Darlene almost growled. "Go strictly by the book. The chances of botulism are tiny."

With a nod from Dr. James, Jim went to open the doors to allow people in. On his own, he limited it to two families at a time. Darlene was kept busy grinding the wheat into flour, but she kept a weather eye on the distribution.

Darlene expected, and heard, a few complaints about both the selection and quantities available, but said nothing, knowing she wouldn't particularly want to live on what she was providing, but knew she could and would if need be.

She was disappointed at the number of people that accepted the handouts. Only a handful declined to take anything other than some of the candy if they had children. It was a real treat for them and the parents voiced their appreciation, unlike the majority.

There were only a couple of cases of meat and vegetables left, but most of the second buckets each of the rice, beans, and lentils. Two-thirds of the buckets of honey and sugar, with several of the small bottles of canola oil, and a dozen of the small camper's size salt shakers, made up the remainder.

The two women on the council hurried home to get containers and then got their shares. Jayne said, "I'll take out my share and put the rest away, if the rest of you want to take off. You have the keys to the storeroom, Doctor?"

"Not on your life!" Darlene said. "You take yours now, like the rest. And then I'll see that the remainder goes under lock and key."

Jayne stomped off to her and Kevin's living quarters in the community center, and returned with containers for her and Kevin's portions. Kevin was with her and carried the items back with her.

"Well," Dr. James said as he, Bear, and Jim helped Darlene close up the open containers. "That went relatively well. Jim, Bear? I noticed you didn't take any."

"Got what I need," Jim said. "I pay my way. And, you didn't take any, either."

"I'm the same way. Darlene, I'd like to buy my portion. What is it worth?"

Darlene didn't hesitate. "Easy. A full day's work. And I'll throw in a little fresh vegetables and some canned fruit. Add a couple jars of chicken." Darlene thought he was going to refuse the extras, but after some hesitation, he nodded.

"Keep a good account. I'm not very good at remembering things like that."

"Oh, be assured. I will. I have my tally book with what everyone owes me." She took a slim leather bound book from her hip pocket and showed it to Dr. James and then put it back.

"Smart," said Dr. James as he locked up the store room and put the key in his pocket.

Darlene started to pick up the box with the grain grinder in it, but Bear beat her to it and carried it out to the truck for her as Jim and the Doctor tagged along. All three noticed the heavier snow and higher wind.

"I think we did this just in time," Jim said, studying the sky. "We're in for another big blow unless I miss my guess."

"I think you're right, Jim," Darlene said. She turned to the Doctor. "I'll get your things together and bring them over to your house in a few minutes."

"I can help," Dr. James said, drawing a rather droll look from Darlene. "Or not," he said.

Jim was right. It was a big blow. The worst of the winter. But it was also the last major storm of the winter. March brought warming temperatures and melting snow, though the process was slow. As soon as the snow melted under the large sheets of black plastic Darlene had staked down on her house lot and the vacant lot, she began to till the soil in anticipation of spring planting. The snow was still several feet deep everywhere except for her property.

Darlene didn't stop with her regular garden plot. She tilled every unused foot of the back yard, front yard, and most of the area of the vacant lot.

The houses in the tract had been built to new 'green' standards in terms of insulation and energy efficient appliances. Darlene still had a full tanker of propane sitting on the lot when the last of the snow melted away.

Taking the standard payment of promised labor, she began to refill the residents' tanks as they went empty one shortly after the other. Those houses where there were children ran out first.

With the distances that needed to be traveled for any purpose, Darlene hadn't used the snowmobiles much, but she stored them for the summer under their covers on the vacant lot, as soon as she thought she could get the Chevy out of the tract.

She was the first one to brave it, while the snow was still around, and went to check the local area for any changes. There were some. Many buildings had their roofs inside. The thick, heavy snow pack had done in long-span roofs. Darlene was sure that if Bear and Jim hadn't kept the community center's roof clear of the snow it would have succumbed, too.

With an eye on future salvaging opportunities, Darlene went well past the points she'd gone before winter. There was still a lot to be salvaged, but the sub-zero temperatures had ruptured essentially all wet pack canned and bottled foods. Making a wide circle Darlene went back to the tract worried about there being enough food to go around again if some of the people in the tract didn't contribute more to their long term survival than they had in the past.

Only a handful, including Bear, Jim, Craig, and Travis had made any attempt the year before to grow gardens. At least this year a handful of families were speaking about putting in gardens. If they had help. That would be her first priority. Second would be large stock and a means to keep it year round. It would take a tremendous number of rabbits, fish, and chicken to keep everyone in high grade protein. Large stock was the only way for long term success. And it just might not be doable.

When she made it back, late that evening, she found half a dozen people anxiously waiting outside her fence line. She used the remote to open the driveway gate and drove in, closing the gate behind her.

"What's going on?" she asked, walking over to the group after she got out of the truck.

"You're back!" someone called.

"Yes, I'm back," Darlene said. "Why wouldn't I be?"

There was quite a bit of mumbling among the small group, but no one spoke up. One possibility of what they were doing suddenly came to her and she went cold, and then hot, suddenly livid at the prospect.

As casually as she could, which wasn't very, Darlene said, "I hope no one was intending to enter my place, thinking I was gone for good. It would be very hazardous for their health. The old laws about not having deadly booby traps no longer apply. It would be a shame if someone lost their life looking for a can of beans, now, wouldn't it?"

There were no replies and the crowd quickly broke up, everyone going their way. Except Dr. James. "I really hope you weren't an active part of this," Darlene said. She felt hurt that he was in the group.

"I was trying to get everyone to go away. What's yours is yours. I just wasn't having much success."

Darlene felt a huge sense of relief, and sighed. "Looks like I'm going to have to hire a guard to watch the place when I leave."

"You really don't need to, do you? You think someone would actually try to get in?"

"Some people already tried, back last year. With things going to get as desperate as they are, I can almost guarantee an attempt in the future."

"Desperate?" Dr. James asked. "Things should be much better now that winter is past us."

"Got another coming up fast, Doc. And I wasn't lying when I said I couldn't support everyone for long term. If we don't get people hustling, and I mean really hustling, we aren't going to be as lucky as we were this past winter. People are going to die."

"It wasn't luck," Dr. James said. "It was you that prevented any deaths."

"Maybe. But I don't plan to be as generous as I was." She glared at the Doctor when he chuckled.

"Laugh if you want, but I mean it. When I don't have much left, I'm going to take care of myself and the rest can go hang."

"Okay. I'm sorry. What do you suggest we do?"

"Gardens, gardens, gardens. Can, can, can. Grow everything possible and home can it for the winter. Stay on reduced, though not subsistence, rations, as people working need more calories, to conserve just that much more for winter. Just had a thought. With so few people knowing how to home can, and the dearth of supplies, I think we'd better figure on freezing much of what we grow, rather than can."

"How on earth do we do that? The freezers in these homes aren't that large. And no one really has the electrical capacity to run them enough to actually freeze things from scratch."

"Don't worry. I'll take care of the means to freeze and store foods suitable for freezing. When can you give me some of those labor hours?"

"Pretty much any time. We've been very fortunate that there hasn't been much illness or injury during all this. I have time on my hands."

"Not anymore," Darlene replied. "Be ready to go tomorrow at nine. I've got a couple of projects that shouldn't endanger your hands or eyesight."

"You sure do look out for me," Dr. James said with a smile.

"Yeah. Doctors are a valuable asset. Might need to trade you off for a milk cow this summer." Darlene was actually smiling and the Doctor laughed.

"Funny. Okay. I'll be ready."

Darlene spent the evening with a map, regional yellow pages, her journal, and the laptop computer. She had plans printed out for the next several weeks that would keep busy anyone that wanted the benefits of working for her.

The first order of business was to get the equipment and supplies needed for everyone to garden. With the trailer behind the Chevy, and Dr. James riding shotgun, Darlene went on a salvaging frenzy. Dr. James, with another crash course in driving something he'd never driven before, transferred two Kubota estate tractors with gardening implements to the tract. One for her use and one for community use.

That got things started. With the most difficult work done mechanically, many of the residents, having learned their lesson, or at least some of it, took to the planting and then care of their gardens with real enthusiasm. Like Darlene, most put in a backyard garden and a front yard garden.

Darlene kept her non-hybrid seeds in reserve. There was no good reason not to use up the hybrid seeds available first. When it came time, Darlene would plant the non-hybrid and collect the seeds for everyone to use.

With the initial flurry of activity in the gardens done, Darlene called in some of the labor obligations owed to her and continued the salvaging. When it came to food she took only half of what was collected, with a quarter going to the community coffers, and those that helped split the other quarter. Going on her salvage trips soon became a favored way to pay back the labor debts.

No so the wood cutting. Despite complaints about cutting more wood when she had quite a bit stacked, and what seemed like an unlimited amount of propane, Darlene put two crews together that weren't likely to do more damage to themselves than the trees they were cutting down. When the vacant lot was filled up to the edges of the garden with cut, split, and stacked firewood, she kept the crews working in the coolness of the spring. The split wood was stored, covered, on several flatbed semi-trailers that disappeared occasionally, usually when Darlene disappeared for a while.

Summer limped in, late and cool. Bear and Jim trained several people to drive semi-tractor trailers and the salvage parties went long distances, with a couple of motorhomes along for people to stay out for several days at a time.

The majority of people, including Dr. James and even Bear, felt like things were going great and that even a winter like the previous one would be handled with ease. Only Jim seemed to notice how frenetic Darlene was to get things done and understand a little of why.

There were few dissenting votes when Darlene asked to buy all the empty houses and lots in the tract. Over Jayne's objections, it was even agreed that she could have them for the things she had already contributed to the community so far that spring and early summer.

Craig, Travis, and two other workers, a husband and wife team, spent long, tiring hours putting up heavy fencing on two adjoining lots that didn't have any. Then she had them gutting the houses, taking out most of the non-load-bearing walls. The heat system was left, along with a way to get water, but both were protected with stout enclosures.

When she and Bear showed up with a stock trailer of cattle and pigs, it became clear what the fences and converted houses were now. Barns and barnyards. Several semi-trailer loads of hay, straw, and grain were brought to the tract and parked on another of Darlene's unoccupied lots.

Darlene had cleared out every farm store and feed and grain business for miles. Concerned about snow accumulations, without the empty lots to dump it in, Darlene worked with Bear and Jim to cut a direct path to the park and lake. The snow would be dumped into the lake during the winter. In the summer the already fenced park would become the grazing grounds for the large stock.

An entire library's content of farming and ranching books were obtained and three families agreed to take over the running of the 'farm' for Darlene, for a share of the production.

With the success she'd had with the rabbits, chicken, and fish, Darlene helped three of the families that had suffered the most the previous winter set up their own operations, providing the initial breeding animals for each of them. Again, in return for more labor from them.

With the gardens doing well, considering the cool temperatures and watery sunlight, people finally had eaten enough to feel comfortable, or more, and wanted to know Darlene's plan to freeze the foods for storage.

"Geez!" Bear said, slapping himself on the head. "That's so simple! Why didn't I think of that?" Darlene and Dr. James, now quite comfortable behind the wheel of a big rig, parked four big reefer trailers alongside the community center. All had propane powered refrigeration units and were quickly plumbed to the community center's propane tank for stationary use.

"Figure one for refrigerator use, and one for deep freeze, with two spares. We picked up more oil and filters for the compressor engines. With luck, they'll last for several years each if taken care of dutifully," Darlene explained.

To Dr. James, Jim, and Bear, Darlene still looked worried about something. Finally, they managed to get her to sit down and talk to them.

"What's going on, Darlene?" asked Bear. "You look like you're still on pins and needles. The way we're set up now, we shouldn't have a problem this winter."

"If we get to keep it," Darlene replied.

"What on earth do you mean?" Dr. James asked.

"One of the small communities like ours about three hundred miles away suddenly went off the air. I'm afraid there is a rogue group out there somewhere preying on those that have managed to survive. If they show up here… There's maybe ten guns in the place, besides what I have, and I can only shoot one… well… two, at a time. I don't think I can defend us against a real attack by even moderately well-armed small group."

"You aren't responsible for the security of this group alone," Jim said. "I'm a part of that, too. Just never really brought it up before. I've got more than just the Glock on my hip."

"And I'll certainly lend a hand," Bear said. "Defense of my family, and therefore this community is paramount, in my opinion. We've made a place for ourselves here. I aim to keep it."

"I'm afraid… I could pass the ammunition, I suppose," Dr. James said. "I don't know if I could use a gun against another human being."

"That's okay," Darlene said, rather surprising the others. "Not everyone is cut out to be a shooter, or even hunter, much less soldier."

She looked at them in turn. "How many do you think would come forward and train to use a weapon and pull watch duty effectively?"

"I think there would be several if you lay it out to the others, the way you have us," Bear said.

"I think it would be better if Doc brings it up, kind of on his own, at the next town hall meeting, without reference to me," Darlene said.

"She's got a point," admitted Jim. "Though there are several more converts to her way of thinking, there is still a hard core element that if she says yea, they say nay, just to oppose her."

"Okay. I can see that," Dr. James said. "I'll bring it up without mentioning Darlene."

"The problem is going to be," Bear said, "Arming people. I've got an old single shot shotgun my father left me, but that's not really suitable to repel an attack by several people."

"Take my word for it, giving everyone a gun that we can train to shoot is not a problem. Nor is ammunition."

Jim was grinning. "I wondered who had hit the gun stores and pawn shops so methodically."

"Matter of self-defense that doesn't seem to have worked," Darlene replied. "No trouble locally, but just like gun control, before, no matter how much you suppress locally, there are always outsiders that are armed that pose a threat."

"Too true," Jim said. "So, we can effectively arm those we train. And Doc is going to broach the subject. What do we do if we don't get any volunteers?"

"I don't know about anyone else," Darlene said, "but I hunker down and protect myself by every means available."

"Wait a minute," Dr. James suddenly said. "How will they, if there is a 'they', even know about us? Much less be able to find us? Our only contact with others has been by radio."

"I've been very careful about communications for this very reason. But someone that listens for very long will pick up the occasional fact here and there, and if they have a keen mind, they can eventually come up with a location. I can't say positively that there is a gang, or that they will show up, but if we don't prepare, if they do, the majority of people here are doomed."

"Okay. When do you think they might attack?" Jim asked.

"Just before winter sets in. I figure they've cleaned out the Coventry group during the winter and will march on, living on what they can salvage in areas where there are no survivors. But they'll want to be somewhere for winter that has the resources to carry them through.

"There could be other options for them, like setting up like we did initially, if they find a good spot with things they can salvage. But if they wait long, they won't have time to set up themselves before winter sets in. They'll most likely make for an established place. I've heard that once you taste the advantages of taking rather than working, the habit is hard to break, no matter what the possible consequences."

"As much as I hate to say it," Jim said, "it could come down to a core group willing to do what's necessary, and let the other's suffer the consequences of doing nothing. Much as Darlene said she would do." Looking at her he added, "But even a small cohesive group had a much better chance of triumphing than a lone person."

"Point taken," Darlene said. "Anyone that wants to join my personal efforts in this matter can. It would be so much better if the entire tract was behind it."

"I'll do my best," Dr. James said.

Dr. James called for a town meeting two days hence. The majority of people showed up, wondering about the solemn tones that had been used when they were contacted.

He laid it all out for them. That the community fight as one, or everyone fight alone."

"But we don't even know they are coming?" protested Jayne. "And even if they do, wouldn't it be better to bargain with them? Perhaps give them some supplies to make it through the winter somewhere around here? They should leave us alone if we do that. That would be so much more logical."

There were some murmuring agreement voices. Darlene kept quiet. Anything she said would only be taken as a challenge and Jayne would fight all the harder. And no one in their right mind wanted to go into battle. Not even Darlene.

But four men stood up, and two women, saying they would help defend the place. Jim and Bear stood up behind the council table, and then Craig and Travis stood up. Darlene saw a couple more men start to rise, but a wife's hand on the shoulder sat them back down before they could rise up all the way.

Darlene was pleased. It was a much better result than she expected. "Maybe I am too cynical," she told herself.

Jayne then protested that women shouldn't be expected to fight.

That's when Darlene stepped forward and said, "I'm in." Jayne didn't voice an objection.

"We'd better go ahead and get an official vote on this," Dr. James said.

Bear immediately said, "I move we form ourselves a militia."

Dr. James reworded it slightly. "All those in favor of training and equipping a self-defense force please raise your hand."

Several people counted the hands and shouted out the number. Dr. James asked for those opposed, since it was going to be close. Very close. The council was tied as well as the community. It was up to Dr. James. After a very long pause, he said. "I vote to raise the defense force." He tapped the gavel on the sounding block and added, "Motion passes. Everyone interested please stay. The rest of you can go home."

Jayne kept her seat as the other two women on the council, both her friends, hurried out. "Are you implying by your presence that you intend to participate in the defense force?" Jim asked.

"Of course not! But someone has to keep an eye on this. With her involved there is the possibility of some type of coup…"

"Get out," Dr. James said. He was obviously angry. "If you are not going to arm yourself to defend your own life, let us that are willing to defend it for you get to business."

With a huff Jayne got up and stomped out. A few seconds later he asked, "Okay. What now?"

"Jim," Darlene said, "You seem to know what's what. Why don't you take charge?"

"Sure thing. Just like back in the Army," he said with a smile. "How many of you have military experience?"

Everyone looked around at one another, but no one spoke up."

"O Kay. That makes it simpler and harder at the same time. Simpler," Jim said, "since you're clean slates and don't have to unlearn anything before you learn my way of doing things. And harder, because there are a lot of basics to learn that wouldn't be necessary if there were some with experience. So be it. Tomorrow. At noon. Here at the community center. That's all for now."

With Darlene, Dr. James, Bear, and Jim staying behind, the others left.

"We have the start of an effective group," Jim said when the door closed. "Everyone looked interested and willing. But not that dangerous eagerness of one just looking for the chance to kill someone."

"When do you want to see the guns?" Darlene asked.

"Day after tomorrow. Tomorrow we just go over the tract and get everyone familiar with the strong points and weak points. I've got a lot of work to do tonight. I'll see you all tomorrow, at Noon."

Bear followed him out, the two talking earnestly. Darlene turned to Dr. James. "Well, Doc, you change your mind about just handing out ammunition?"

"In a sense. I'm not sure I could use a gun against a human being, but I want to have the option of the knowledge and equipment to do it, if I ever do decide to do it."

"Good for you. With that, I'll leave you. Good night."

Darlene headed for the door as Dr. James watched. He shook his head and turned back to the pad on the table in front of him when she left the room by the side door.

Pedaling the Paratrooper bike easily, Darlene went home. She wanted to go over the list of arms and ammunition she'd salvaged.

CHAPTER SIX

-

Jim didn't have the group do much PT. All were fairly fit and lean from the hard work and healthy diet. He was, like Darlene, a planner. With everyone fully cognizant of the ground they would be protecting, Jim said, "The reason I wanted to stress this so much is the fact that if an assault team makes it into the tract, and it goes house to house, we don't have a chance. Most of the residents will die. I don't plan on letting that happen. I want you to spend the rest of the day going over this tract on your own, or in teams, to decide what you would do if an enemy team tried to get in what have been pointed out as weak points. Tomorrow at nine. Here at the community center."

Most of the others paired up, though Bear went out on his own. So did Darlene. She'd been all over the tract, but had only had a few thoughts about defending it completely. Most of her defense measures were concerned with her home.

That evening Darlene unlocked and went into the shelter. She went through the inventory of weapons and ammunition and set aside the ones she would take to the community center the next morning.

She was loading them up when Dr. James stopped on his way to the community center. He looked at the back of the pickup at the cases of ammunition and the carefully stacked long arms on soft blankets. "Did you really loot all of those from gun stores?"

"Not loot. Salvage. There's a difference. But yes. And pawn shops, and some private residences, based on the stores' 4473's."

"4473's?" the Doctor asked as he slid into the passenger seat of the truck at Darlene's hand motion.

"The purchase papers a person has to fill out and sign to buy a gun. The dealer keeps them pretty much forever, unless the BATFE comes through and takes possession of them."

"I see. And you checked through all of them? To find more guns?"

"First I went through the stores' sales records, referenced the 4473 form number for the gun I wanted, and then took the address off the form and went looking."

"I see. Simple. If you know the procedure."

"Yep. Here we are. You want to grab a case of the 5.56?"

"Uh… which one… Oh. I see. It's on the case."

"Yep, again." Darlene grabbed four weapons and headed for the open door of the community center. The rest of the self-defense force was there. All hurried to help bring in the rest of the weapons and ammunition.

Other than Jim, Bear, and Dr. James, who had some idea of what Darlene might have, the others were amazed. "Got 5.56, 7.62x39, 7.62x51, 12-gauge, 9mm, and .45 ACP. Figured to keep it simple and semi-auto for the rifles and pistols, and pump shotguns. Military calibers and gauges only." She listed the numbers of each of the different weapons she had."

"Well, right off the bat, no 7.62x39," Jim said. "No need to have more variations than necessary. Or magazines. That leaves out everything but M-16 pattern carbines, and the HK-91or PTR-91 rifles. You have more of them and only a couple of each of the others. How you fixed on magazines for those two groups?"

"Good. Enough for several for each rifle. More, even."

"Probably stick with the 870 pumps. Probably only two or three. You have more than that one?"

"Yep. Several."

"What's the magazine situation on the handguns? Especially the Beretta 92's, Colt M-1911's, and Glock 17's & 21's?"

"Again, plenty of each. There are a few extended magazines for the G17's."

"Won't need them. Complicates things too much. Everyone will shoot each type of weapon and decide what's best for you. Let's load up and go down to lake."

Everything was loaded back into Darlene's pickup, and everyone climbed in the back. It was a short trip and Darlene stopped when Jim asked her to.

"Not the best range, and won't do for training, but it'll work to try the guns out. Just aim for the waterline on the far side of the lake. Let's go through the safety rules."

Jim kept it simple and soon was loading up a Bushmaster M-4 style carbine. Everyone shot it in turn. Then each of the other guns. Jim was watching carefully and had his mind made up what each person would probably want. He was right. Each one stated the weapon he or she wanted and they were the ones Jim thought they would pick.

There was an equal mix of the M-4 style carbines and HK-91/PTR-91 rifles, but the handguns ran the gamut. Only Dr. James wanted one of the shotguns.

"Okay," Jim said, "Your choices are fine. We have good magazine interchangeability for the rifles, where it's really important. The handguns don't matter that much." Jim turned to Darlene. "Would you take back what we don't need and pick up what we do? Meet us back at the community center. Oh. Any load bearing gear? And cleaning gear?"

"All different kinds. I'll bring something for each weapon."

"Okay. You want some help?"

"I think so. Doc?"

A very surprised Dr. James got into the truck and rode back to Darlene's house, getting out of the truck and following her into the garage carrying the guns that weren't needed, after she opened the walk door security shutter. "In here," she said, opening the first of the doors into the shelter.

"This… This is a shelter, isn't it?" Dr. James asked.

"Yes, it is. And I expect you to keep it to yourself. Also what it now contains." She opened the other door and stepped inside. Guns and ammunition, web and leather gear, and case after case of ammunition were stacked everywhere.

"You have enough for a small army here!" Dr. James exclaimed.

"Most of this isn't suitable for an army. But I didn't want it falling into hands that could turn it on me. And I wanted to preserve what I could. It still irks me I haven't gone back and done a few historical salvage runs."

"You intend to gather up historical materials?"

"Yes." She looked over at him in the light from the LED fixtures. "Does that surprise you?"

"Actually. No, it doesn't, believe it or not. You're a very… unique… woman."

"Yeah. Here." She handed him a rifle, and then another. "Be careful with them."

With Dr. James carrying out the things that Darlene selected from the various stacks, they soon had what they needed and the two went to the community center. Everyone picked up their weapons of choice and went through the load bearing equipment, taking items appropriate to their choice of weapons.

She'd found several mall ninja people that had all kinds of military style gear for show. Some of it was even pretty good equipment. That's what Darlene handed out. Jim soon had them stripping down their weapons and cleaning them thoroughly to get familiar with them.

Next was setting up the support equipment, getting each one comfortable in their individual gear arrangements. Darlene had brought several of the FRS radios she'd acquired and Jim issued everyone one of them and they set the frequencies they would use.

They broke at noon. Jim insisted that the weapons be locked up in the community center until they each had a chance to practice with them so there would be no accidents. "Tomorrow. Again at nine. We'll go to the nearest safe range so figure out transport."

"Not doing anything else today?" Bear asked.

"No," Jim replied. "I and everyone else have chores to do. This is all extra, in addition to regular activities." He said it more for the others' benefit than Bear's, and all got the message.

For three consecutive days the routine was the same. Shooting practice at a nearby spot that had an overpass ramp to act as a backstop. After that, everyone was told to keep their weapons and radio handy, and practice once a week with them, and practice defensive tactics together in the tract once a week.

Darlene looked much more relaxed once the self-defense force became a cohesive working group.

The summer turned out to be hardly summer at all, but a continuation of spring and an early fall. But the gardens had produced and the reefers were filling up nicely. When it was time to butcher the stock that wouldn't winter over, it was a community undertaking. At least for the most part. Children and their attendant teenage babysitters were exempted. A handful of others opted out of the operation, volunteering to do other duties. Even Kevin pitched in. Only Jayne refused to do anything during that time.

Kevin and Jayne were back in their own home, the generator finally replaced. All the small generators had been used hard, and most were replaced that summer with larger, propane fired generators that Darlene had found at another propane place. Still couldn't run them continuously like Darlene could hers, but they would hold up better under use, and provided more power, to boot.

The snows started again, in late October, but weren't as massive as the previous year's first snows. There was only two feet on the ground at Thanksgiving, and the community had a real Thanksgiving Day feast, minus a few traditional food items. There was even a hotly contested touch football game played.

Darlene went home that evening feeling like her worries about a band of plunderers was misplaced. The major snows were just days away. She'd been taking a snowmobile out around the track ever since the snow started sticking. She could see any tracks in the fresh snow easily now. The only tracks she saw were animal tracks as animals repopulated from lesser damaged areas to territory lying unclaimed by any of their kind.

"Things might just go fine this winter!" she said softly as she fell asleep. She couldn't have been more wrong.

There was contention in the group, many wanting to turn back to the last good place they'd settled for a while during the summer. An area not as salvaged out as some. But their leader was adamant. There was a prize for the taking not too far ahead of them. It was well worth some hardship to get to for wintering over.

There were thirty-nine of them. Twenty-five fighting men, eight women the men shared, and six minor children the women had managed to protect from the assaults of the men when drunk.

The smell of the side of beef roasting over a wood fire had traveled for miles on the light breeze that was blowing from the tract to where the group had camped the night before. Like dogs scenting a helpless animal of prey, the men's noses twitched at the tantalizing smells. There was no longer any dissent. All were eager to move forward the next morning.

Even Darlene admitted it was sheer luck that she spotted the group approaching during one of her outside-the-tract snowmobile runs as she was coming back home. The snow had started again and any tracks would soon be covered. As soon as she saw them, they saw her, as they were looking for where the sounds of the snowmobile were coming from.

She gunned the snowmobile, but not before one of the men got off a lucky shot. She felt the fire in her leg, but leaned low and took up a zigzag course, traveling as fast as she'd ever dared go before on the powerful machine.

Their usual method of scouting out a neighborhood or compound from a distance and then striking when the weaknesses were known now unusable, the leader called for an immediate attack, following the snowmobile trail. And the blood trail of lone spots of blood every few meters.

With a yell for the women to set up camp, the leader and the others dropped everything but weapons and ammunition and began to lope along the trail.

Darlene stopped when she was sure she was out of sight and used her FRS radio to notify Jim of the situation. Fighting off dizziness she waited where she was until the men came into sight. She gunned the snowmobile again, quickly out of sight once more, but not before another shot whizzed past her left ear.

"Geez!" she muttered and kept the snowmobile at a slow pace, to keep out of sight, yet temptingly close for the men to keep after her.

The big drift at the tract entrance was already four feet high with the snow that had already fallen. Darlene rode up and over it and almost ran over Jim. She swerved and stopped the snowmobile.

"They're right behind me!" she said as she struggled off the snowmobile. She always carried her Marlin and the Redhawk when she was off the property, still more comfortable with them than she was the heavy PTR-91 she'd chosen as her tract defense weapon.

She brought the Marlin down off her back and limped up to the guardhouse, filling in Jim on what she'd seen. "There's at least thirty of them. Men and women. But I don't think any of the women are coming after me. Just the men."

"I've got everyone lined up at the wall here by the street, with three people laying back as a last guard at the community center. Everyone is gathered there. A couple more people took radios and went out to watch the walls in other directions, just in case. People really pulled together when your radio call came in and said what was happening."

"Okay, good." Darlene blinked her eyes and swayed. Only then did Jim notice the blood running down the leg of her snowmobile suit.

"You're hurt! I'll get the Doc!"

Darlene grabbed his arm. "No! We need every gun on the line. It'll wait." Under her breath she added, "I hope."

Leaning against the back of the guard shack, Darlene raised the Marlin up and levered a round into the chamber. She had to blink her eyes several times to get her vision to clear enough to take aim at the first figure to appear.

The men were spread in a long line, the slowest at the rear, here and there two abreast. Had the battle been the other way around, it would have been called a massacre. Since it was the bad guys that died it was simply a good defensive action.

The rest of the self-defense force had been ordered to wait until Jim gave the word to fire, but when Darlene fired first, they all rose up from behind the fence and cut loose. Jim knew it wasn't particularly well aimed fire, considering the large number of rounds expended versus the number of holes in the dead, but it was still effective.

Darlene's first three shots scored devastating hits on the three men in the lead of the attack. Her next shot went into the snow at her feet as she fell over sideways, unconscious.

Unlike Darlene, who had started at the front of the line, Jim took careful aim and began dropping the men at the rear of the group, from his position alongside the edge of the fence, on the side opposite the guardhouse from Darlene.

When all the attackers were down, Jim signaled and Bear and Travis, guns on point, went out to check the bodies. In a few minutes of tense silence Bear called out, "All dead."

Jim yelled back, "Strip them of weapons anyway and get back in here." He turned to Craig and one of the women defenders nearest him on the fence. "Go get a couple more snowmobiles."

Both jumped own off their perches that had been installed at several places along the wall and ran off, disappearing into the much harder snowfall that was coming down now.

Bear and Travis made it back to Jim about the time Craig and Colleen got there with the snowmobiles. With a gunner holding on tightly behind the drivers, Jim, Bear, and Craig, with the three others, took off to back track the attackers.

They found the women and children on the run away from the tract. They'd never even tried to set up a camp, choosing even the slightest chance of freedom over the surety of a vassal life with the men that had captured them.

Approaching quickly but cautiously, Jim cut in front of the tightly spaced group, the children surrounded by the women. It didn't take long for Jim to determine the facts of the matter and get the group turned around, headed back to the safety of the tract.

They shied away from the bodies slowly being covered with snow, except for a quick step close to spit on a particularly hated abuser.

With assurance that all the adult males had been killed, Jim called all but one of his small force down off the wall. He wasn't willing to leave the gate untended, just in case. The rather joyous group headed for the community building.

It was only after Dr. James had finished his quick examination of the women and children for immediate needs and communicable diseases did he ask about Darlene. Jim looked horrified suddenly.

"I forgot her! She'd been shot when she ran into them and was bleeding badly! She told me not to worry and joined into the fight.

Jim, Bear, and Dr. James rushed out of the community building, leaving the newcomers in the capable hands of the rest of the self-defense force, minus the one at the gate. And Darlene. They rode the snowmobiles faster than was safe, but they got to the guard shack in record time.

"Where is she?" Dr. James yelled.

"Here! Here!" Jim called. Darlene was almost covered by the snow, an ominous amount of it bright red beside her left thigh.

"Help me get her up," Dr. James said. Her head lolled limply when they got her up. Between them and the snowmobiles, they got her to Dr. James house, then inside, and on the bed in the second bedroom.

"Bear! Get your wife! I need her. Jim. You keep an eye on things out there, will you? I don't want anything going on while I work on her. She's lost a lot of blood and the bullet is still in her."

The two rushed off and Dr. James got Darlene's snowmobile suit off, then her jeans, and covered her with a blanket, leaving the bullet wound uncovered. He noticed the healed bullet wound just inches from the new one, and then ran out of the room. He was coming back into the room with his medical bag when Julie Johanovich came in.

She took a look, and with the practiced ease of the professional nurse that she was, began to assist Dr. James in his treatment of Darlene.

Two days later, while Dr. James was napping in a chair by her bedside, Darlene woke up with a groan. "Where am I? Did we get them all? I think I've been shot." Her voice was weak, but Dr. James heard her. He stood up and pulled the stethoscope from around his neck and began to check her vitals.

"You're in my second bedroom," the Doctor explained as he continued to check her heart, despite her weak efforts to prevent him from putting the stethoscope on her chest. "We got them all. Brought in some badly used women and children. Yes, you've been shot. And if I'm any kind of doctor, you narrowly missed getting pneumonia, lying out there in the snow as long as you did, already weak from loss of blood."

Darlene yanked the blanket back up to her chin when the Doctor finished what he was doing. "Can I have some water? My mouth feels like a desert."

"Of course." Dr. James helped her hold the glass from the bedside table to her lips when she quickly discovered she didn't have the strength to do it alone.

"Uh... I need the bathroom now," she said after swallowing only a few sips. "But there is no way..."

"I'll get Julie to help you. Just hold it a minute."

Julie was asleep on the sofa in Dr. James' living room. He wakened her gently and she immediately came to. "What is it? How is she?"

"She needs to go to the bathroom. I… uh… don't think it would be a good idea if I tried to help her."

"Obviously not, Doctor."

He waited out of the line of sight between the second bedroom and the bathroom until Julie called him back to the bedroom.

Darlene was back in the bed, blanket once again up to her chin. "When can I get out of here?"

"A few more days," Dr. James said. "I'm not going to chance you coming down with something in your weakened condition."

"Can't you move me to my place and treat me there? I don't like being in your house."

"Mean's you'd have to let me in, you know. Julie, too. You've been reluctant to have visitors."

Darlene bit her lip. "Yeah… Okay… You and Julie can come in."

"Need someone to help me move you besides Julie."

"Okay, okay. Bear and Jim, too."

"You go get them and I'll get her presentable to move," Julie said. "I'll go get you something to wear from your bedroom."

She really wanted to resist, but she was just too tired. "My keys are in my snowmobile suit. Oh, no! My animals!"

"Ah. Yes," Julie said. "Well, you have to know. Bear has been taking care of them. We found your keys. But he hasn't gone into the house."

"Oh. Tell him I said thank you."

Julie left the room and Darlene fell asleep before she returned with a bundle of clothing in her hands.

"Wake up, sleepyhead," Julie crooned.

Darlene came around slowly. Fortunately, she was slight and Julie was capable. Julie had her dressed in just a couple of minutes and called for Jim and Bear to come in. Taking her up in a fireman's two-man chair carry, they moved her as gently as they could to her bedroom, with Julie leading and Dr. James following. Julie held the door as the two men took her through, and then shooed them out of the bedroom when they set her down on the edge of the bed.

Darlene was tired and hurting when she was finally ensconced comfortably in her bed. "Ok, Doctor," Julie called, "You can come in now."

Dr. James came in and gave Darlene another examination. She didn't have the strength to resist. "That was almost too much for you," he said. "I'm going to have Julie give you something for the pain and another dose of antibiotics. One of us will be close at all times. You're not out of the woods yet."

Darlene didn't respond. She was already asleep. "Hold on the painkiller until she asks for it," Dr. James said. "I don't want to drug her up too much. I don't think she particularly likes being treated at all."

"She's a very self-sufficient, capable woman," Julie said, taking a paperback book from the pocket of her sweater. She sat down in the chair she moved to the head of the bed. "I'll keep an eye on her for a while if you want to go get some real sleep."

"Yeah. Probably should. I'm pretty tired, myself." He let himself out, talked to Bear and Jim for a minute, and then went to his own home to get some sleep.

"You know," Jim told Bear, "I think the Doc is rather taken with Darlene."

"I'm coming to that conclusion, myself. What do you think she thinks about him?"

"I haven't got a clue," Jim replied, shaking his head. "She plays her cards close to the vest. I can't read her very well about some things." Jim laughed. "Of course, a few other things, there ain't no doubt about it."

Bear laughed too. "Too true."

The two split up, to take care of some of the things that Darlene would be doing if she were able.

Dr. James and Julie found that Darlene was an excellent patient when asleep. Not so much when she was awake. Not that she was demanding, she wasn't… Well, not demanding in terms of treatment and care, but she was having a difficult time not being out and about. Being in the know. She asked questions constantly about the state of this and that, and a few more things.

Dr. James released her much sooner than he would have anyone else. But he'd found her to be highly resilient, and after the first initial problems, she had recovered quickly from the effects of the wound and with the brush with pneumonia. Besides the fact that she was up and dressed, ready to go outside when Julie brought the doctor into the room to see her.

"You should still be in bed," Dr. James said.

"I don't want to be in bed. I'm tired of being in bed. What I need is to get up and do something. Check on my animals. Bear's been doing it, in addition to taking care of his own family. Everyone needs to pull their own weight."

Darlene shut up quickly, not willing to continue and let the Doctor and Julie see how winded the discourse had made her.

"Well, if I can't stop you, at least follow my advice and take it easy. Eat heartily. And get plenty of rest. If you have a problem, any problem at all, sent someone to get me and get back into bed."

"Okay, Doc. I've got it. Eat and sleep. That's what I've been doing. What I need is some fresh air."

"Okay. But I'm warning you," Dr. James said, "I will not be happy if you wind up with pneumonia, despite my best efforts of preventing it."

Discerning some real concern in his voice and manner, Darlene eased up a bit. "Okay, Doc. I promise. I'll be careful and not over do it."

"Good. Thank you. I guess I'll leave you to your own devices for a while."

Julie waited until she heard the front door close before she asked Darlene, "You ready to lay back down now?"

"Uh… Yeah. I think I will. I'll check on the animals in a little while."

"I thought you might. I'll have lunch ready at noon. Try to be up by then." Darlene was already asleep before Julie finished her sentence.

Julie left to see about her own family, but was back to prepare a hot lunch for Darlene when she woke up, shortly after one in the afternoon. Rather groggy, and occasionally leaning against the wall for support, Darlene followed her nose to the kitchen, the smell of the hearty stew causing her mouth to water.

"I'm afraid I tended to the greenhouse and picked a few fresh things to make your soup. Hope you don't mind." Julie glanced over at Darlene.

Darlene frowned for a brief instant. But what could she say. Bear and Julie, and even the Doctor, were doing the best they could to help her. She shouldn't make it any more difficult that it already was.

"It's okay. Everyone has to know about it by now, anyway, unless they're dense as a rock." She took a seat and let Julie fuss over her. Feeling much stronger, Darlene went out into the back yard and looked around.

Bear was there checking on Darlene's small stock. "I hate to ask, Bear, since you've already done so much, but have you checked on the fish in the garage?"

"Sure did. Took a couple of days for it to dawn on me that you had to have a tank somewhere, since you have a constant supply of fresh fish. I wasn't snooping, but I had to check, and found the tank in the garage. Man, those fish go crazy when they get fed worms."

Darlene smiled. "Sure do." She cut her trip outside short and went back inside, satisfied that Bear was more than capable of handling things, and, more importantly, willing.

It was a month before Darlene was back to her old self. Only it wasn't quite her old self. She was a bit more open about things and invited all those that had helped out at her place over for dinner. She'd thought about trying to get them to take something in pay for what they'd done, but had enough sense to do the dinner, instead.

She even kept her cool when she found out that the newcomers were now ensconced in the remaining three houses that Darlene had bought from the community. "I guess we had to put them somewhere," she said after the first flash of anger. "They getting enough to eat?"

Dr. James nodded. "We're feeding them out of the community coffers that you were such a big help in providing. Even with a long winter, we should still make out okay." Darlene nodded.

After the dinner, the others thanked Darlene and headed for their own homes. The snow was coming down hard and everyone wanted to get home before the streets became impassable until they could be cleared.

Dr. James was the last one, and even offered to help with the dishes. To his surprise, Darlene agreed. As they worked in the kitchen, Darlene said, "I was on the radio a lot while I was recuperating, and I think a couple of the nearer communities to us are willing to do some trading with us. There is still a lot of salvaging to do, but that won't last forever, and though we are in pretty good shape for some things, growing stock feed is beyond our capabilities. At least at the moment. Plus, we need to ensure genetic diversity in our stock, both large and small. We need additional breeding stock, all the way around.

"And biodiesel. We're going to be dependent on it pretty soon. The existing fuel will run out. Besides, it's getting old and I haven't found any PRI-G or PRI-D to freshen it. If we can find some of those products we will have a lot more useable fuel, for a while.

"Some of the other communities have transitioned from barter and trade only, to a partial currency. Gold and silver coins. It looks like I may need to become a banker, too. I have quite a bit of gold and silver myself. I'm thinking about starting to pay people in precious metal coins, to get some in circulation in the community, so people here will be able to trade on an even footing with the other communities."

"You're always thinking, aren't you?" Dr. James said as Darlene handed him a plate to dry.

"I guess so. My ex-husband didn't care for the trait in me." Darlene cut her eyes over to Dr. James and back just as quickly.

"I find it refreshing," the Doctor said and then chuckled. "Most of the time."

"I guess I can be rather off-putting at times…"

"I find it rather endearing…" Slowly Dr. James leaned down slightly, gently taking Darlene's chin to turn her face toward his. She didn't resist or object when he kissed her. In fact, after the first few moments, she was kissing back.

It was some time before Darlene put her hand on Dr. James chest and pushed him slightly away. "Doc… Brian. I'm kind of old fashioned. A kiss is one thing, but I'm not ready for anything else without a minister or justice of the peace being involved."

Dr. James nodded. "I understand. I can wait."

"Yeah. So can I. But finding a minister is top of the list of projects this spring."

They turned back to finish the dishes, and when they were done, Dr. James went home.

It was a tough winter, even longer and colder than the previous winter, though with less snow. The atmosphere was drying out. The seas were withdrawing from the inroads they'd made on the worlds landmasses when the land borne ice had melted. That fresh water was again piling up in the far north and far south as snow and ice, lowering the sea levels over the years below what they were before the meteor strikes.

What had once been extreme winters were to be the norm for generations. Summers were cool, but there were summers. Warm enough and long enough for crops to grow. In the areas that were not encroached on by ice or permanent snow pack, life went on. Even in the 'burbs.

THE END

THANK YOU FOR READING

"DISASTER IN THE BURBS""

By

Jerry D. Young

LIKE THIS BOOK?

See more great books at www.creativetexts.com

"OZARK RETREAT"

"BUGGING HOME"

"THE SLOW ROAD"

"LOW PROFILE"

"RUDY'S PREPAREDNESS SHOP"

"CME: CORONAL MASS EJECTION"

"THE HERMIT"

& MANY MORE GREAT PAW FICTION & OTHER TITLES

THANK YOU!

MEET THE AUTHOR

Jerry D Young was born at home, in Senath, Missouri July 3, 1953. At age 5 the family rented a small farm house on an active farm 40 miles southwest of St. Louis. While the family weren't farmers, they lived something of a homestead type life, raising a milk cow, sometimes two, and calves, a pig or two, chickens, and the occasional goat. Along with the stock, a large garden helped to feed Jerry's three brothers and two sisters for several years. Fishing and hunting contributed to the pantry, as did foraging the wild edibles on the property.

At the age of 14, the family, minus a brother and two sisters that were now adults and on their own, moved back to Senath. Having been encouraged from an early age to read, Jerry was a regular patron of the Senath Branch Library.

A love of a good story was born within him, and shortly before graduating high school, for a lack of stories that he liked at the library, he began to write short vignettes, and started taking notes for stories that he wanted to tell. Jerry eventually began to write in earnest and now has more than 100 titles to his credit including Prep/PAW stories, Action/Adventure, and a few of the romance type stories that first got him started.

Made in the USA
Monee, IL
25 September 2020

43370831R00135